The Moonlight Diner

The Moonlight Diner

D. Allyson Howlett

LUMINARY PUBLISHING HOUSE

ISBN (Ebook): 978-1-968972-22-6

ISBN (Paperback):978-1-968972-07-3

ISBN (Hardcover):978-1-968972-08-0

Cover design by Hollowestudios at http://hollowestudios.com/

To the metal head drifter that stole my good girl heart.

"There is only one race. The human race."

Rosa Parks

Chapter 1
The Drifter

OAK SPRINGS, NEW YORK 1958

This place was a drag. Nobody had been in or out for over an hour. Not many people came by past midnight on an early Tuesday morning. Most had the sense not to drive on a night like this when it was raining cats and dogs big enough to drown Lady Liberty. Oak Springs wasn't a happening place given that it sat right off the highway. You'd drive right past it if you didn't know it was there, but there was nowhere to grab a bite before the long stretch to Albany. They were two different worlds connected only by the shining neon lights of the Moonlight Diner.

All was quiet, except for the rain pattering on the windows running left, right, and center of the L-shaped eatery. The laminate double-seated booths reflected the meager streetlights off their blue and white surface. The checkered floor was shiny and slick from being mopped repeatedly in an effort to eliminate the drag of the late shift.

Prairie rested her chin in the palm of her hand as she stared out into the empty parking lot. Her wavy mahogany hair, that was pulled back by a trio of yellow paper flowers above her right ear, tickled the sides of her freckled cheeks. Her uniform matched the

upholstery and overall color scheme of the diner itself: a pairing her folks hadn't bothered to change in over ten years.

This wasn't where she saw herself after high school. She had wanted to become a nurse at a hospital helping the injured and the sick, but her folks needed her here, working the graveyard shift at the diner. She couldn't say no to them; they needed the help. It had only been a year since she'd graduated, but it felt longer than that. Like she had lost time driving in circles over and over again.

"We are made in the shade tonight, aren't we? Beverly's dark ponytail whipped up the scent of hot coffee through the air as she slid a rag across the speckled countertop. "Can't think of a more exciting place to be than standing 'round here listening to Elliot bash my ears till the sun comes up."

She turned with her brow raised toward the serving window where Elliot's shaggy blonde mop popped into view under his black hair net.

"I heard that." With a disgruntled huff, he turned up the dial on his hand radio attempting to drown out any added trash talk.

"What's got you all fired up?" Prairie smirked, leaning into Bev's arm.

"I just rather be kickin' it with my Georgie, all cozy by his fireplace, watching Jack Benny or Lucy. Heck, I'd even let him watch Gunsmoke if it got me out of a late shift working here."

Prairie shook her head, "You got nothing left to talk about except Georgie since you've been going steady."

"What can I say? He's got me real gone. With them Tony Curtis looks, how could I not be?"

"I swear, Bev, if my daughter grows up to be as fast as you, I'll disown her." Elliot's rusty voice, from puffing too many cigarettes, caused Bev's lips to tighten as her ponytail came across her shoulder. She glared at him from the front of the diner.

"You best shut your trap, Elliot! You don't know nothing about it."

"And I don't want to."

"You think cuz you're married and got kids that you know everything there is to know about love."

"I ain't no square just cuz I've settled down." Elliot replied, adjusting his round specs on his nose.

"You're as square as they come. Four sharp corners and straight sides."

A mention of Oak Springs redirected Prairie's attention to the voice over the radio.

"Stop talking will ya?" Prairie's tone cut through their dirt. "Turn that up, Elliot."

He obliged as both Prairie and Bev leaned towards the now raised voice of the reporter over the air.

"This marks the third death in the recent Route 43 murders outside of Oak Springs. Due to the amount of trauma on the body, the victim has not been identified. The only information we can provide is that he is a white male and about six feet tall. Police say the victim was pulled through the driver side window of his car, dragged about fifty feet into the surrounding forest, and torn apart. There were no weapons or footprints, other than those of the local wildlife found at the scene. A small red handbag was discovered in the backseat, and though a few belongings and change were inside, no ID was found."

Bev shook her head and squinted her eyes, "I don't wanna hear any more of that. How terrible."

"Police are investigating this and using all resources necessary to gather clues as to who or what could be responsible for such a heinous act in our sleepy little corner of New York State . . . "

"Elliot! Don't you have ears?"

With a quick turn, Elliot dumbed down the sound, cutting off any hope of hearing the rest of the report.

"I can't believe there's been another killing around here." Prairie sighed, glancing out the window as if she might see another happening right outside the highway diner.

"It gives me the jitters." Bev shivered and clutched her arms. "How anybody can snuff a person like that . . . it's damn near crazy."

"You better stay close to your beau then, Bev." Elliot snorted as he scraped the grill clean.

Bev rolled her eyes. "Lord only knows how Wanda puts up with you. You must be worth something other than that ring you slid on her finger."

"Keep runnin' your mouth there—"

The jingle of the front door drew their attention. He came in, dark and mysterious like, and drenched from the rain. Rolling over the floor smooth like butter, he slid onto one of the stools at the counter with ease. Prairie watched as his arms crossed in front of him, his leather jacket a few shades darker than his skin.

"Hey, you." Elliott's voice broke the cool silence. "We don't want your kind here."

"Says who?" Prairie shot daggers at him through the serving window.

"There's diners for spooks like him. This ain't one of them."

"Mind your business, Elliot. If he pays, he stays. Keep your trap shut and just do what my daddy pays you to do."

Prairie moved on over to the drifter and leaned against the counter. "Don't mind him. He's just a small-minded imp." Her comment didn't seem to gain a reaction from his brown-eyed glare. Pressing her lips together, she pulled out her pad and pencil from her apron.

"So, what'll it be?"

"Just coffee. Black." His voice was sullen.

"Want me to grab you a towel too? The rain got you pretty good out there."

"No thank you, ma'am." He ran his decorated hand through his dark, pompadour hair, shaking drops in all directions. A round, pale scar lay underneath his left eye. The scar couldn't have been bigger than a dime. Little webs reached out in all directions from it, disappearing into his strong cheekbones and squared jaw.

Prairie wondered how he got that scar and where this man came from. He couldn't be much older than her. He had that greasy look about him, like he was someone who liked causing trouble for people. Hoodlums weren't common in a small town like Oak Springs. They were more of a New York City thing you hear about in the papers or on the radio. She hoped that any trouble he might have been partial to didn't follow him. The last thing this place needed was more trouble keeping customers away.

She turned around to grab a fresh pot. Beverly came beside her and arched an eyebrow towards their newest customer.

"Hush." Prairie whispered as she grabbed a plain mug from the rack, filling it with the bitter, rich liquid.

She took it over and slid him a napkin with the steaming cup. "Here you go."

"Thank you much." He took it with his left hand and brought it up to let the aroma waft into his nostrils. His voice carried a southern drawl, making her think he must have traveled far to find himself in New York.

"Enjoy." Before Prairie could draw away, she noticed red droplets from where his arm had rested. "You're bleeding, sir."

The drifter lowered his mug quickly, wiping the stained water with his jacket sleeve. "It's nothin', ma'am."

"Don't tell me it's nothing." Fishing under the counter, Prairie pulled out a clean cloth and took his arm without asking. She pulled up his jacket and saw his rich dark skin all cut up with small, jagged holes.

Before she could put the cloth to it, he pulled away taking it with him as he stood up from the stool.

"Thank you, I don't mean to trouble ya."

Prairie took a step back, her hands pressing against the rapid thudding of her heart, "No, I. . . I apologize."

They stood in quiet contemplation, looking at each other as if waiting for someone to make a move. Prairie couldn't help but notice the steady caution in his eyes, looking her over like she had an ulterior motive to her kindness. She tried to speak, but her mouth went dry. There was nothing she could say in her startled state. All she could do was watch him, clutching his arm to his chest with the cloth she gave him.

"Everything all right over here?" Beverly's voice broke over them like a rock on the ice.

She came to stand not too far from Prairie: her eyes darting between her and the drifter.

Finally, he dug a fist into his pockets, pulled out a few dimes, and slapped them onto the counter next to the mug of coffee.

"Much appreciated," he glanced at the name sewn into her uniform. "Miss Prairie."

Her name on his lips sent shivers down her spine. Prairie swallowed, lowering her hands to her apron, "You need change?"

"No, thank you, ma'am." He said, tucking the towel into his back pocket. "Have a good night."

He flashed a quick smile and backed up toward the door, pushing it open into the rain. Popping up his collar, he walked down the lit sidewalk and into the night.

Prairie's eyes didn't leave him until Elliot's voice stung at her ears. "Causing trouble did he, Prairie? You just wait till I tell your daddy about this."

She glared at him and grabbed the mug to bring it to the window. "You're not my babysitter, Elliot."

"You'll appreciate me looking out for you more if he is the murderer."

"Well, he isn't." Prairie dropped the mug at the window with a thud and proceeded back to the counter to wipe up any rain left behind.

Prairie noticed some red spots still lingered on its surface. Quick as a whip, she wiped up what remained with the back of her apron.

Beverly came in close to avoid Elliot overhearing. "Was that blood?"

"Yeah . . . his arm was all cut up."

"Prairie." Beverly placed a hand on her shoulder. "You best be careful who you put your hands on."

"He's just a drifter. I doubt we'll ever see him again." The recent murder crept into her mind. How could anyone be sure what type was capable of murder?

Chapter 2
The Rich Boy

"W hat's got you so lip tight?" Billy leaned over in the car as he tore onto the highway.

Prairie shot him a glance and looked into his baby blue eyes, hoping to seem cross with him. "I'm just thinking, is all." She leaned back in the fine leather seat of Billy's Bel Air. It was a lovely late summer afternoon. The wind passed through her hair as they cruised with the top down. It reminded her of her younger years with her folks: driving up to the Hemsworth's lakeside cabin to enjoy a day of sipping on lemonade, fire roasted weenies, and wading in the cool water.

"The only thing you need to be thinkin' about is us getting hitched." Billy smirked, sliding his hand around the wheel.

"Keep dreaming, Billy." Prairie rolled her eyes. "I'm not ready to get married. Especially to you."

"Why not? What's so bad about me?"

Prairie huffed, focusing on his finely combed hair and ironed collared shirt. His pleated trousers and well-polished loafers were as pristine as they had come. Him being a Hemsworth meant he sure could afford it. His family owned the largest manufacturing company in upstate New York specializing in large equipment for businesses and hospitals. There was no denying that having the

family name would come with benefits, but Prairie was never after money nor security. As much as Billy fit the package of what any self-respecting woman was after in a man, she didn't care for it.

Not that Billy wasn't a looker, with his angled face and Cheshire grin that any girl would swoon over.

She was the only girl who ever told him no; the only girl he hadn't stopped trying to get back with once they split after high school.

"There's nothing wrong with you. I'm just not the marrying type."

"Says you. You'll come through. Just like they all do."

Prairie swung a lick across his arm. "Don't you talk to me like that, Billy! I ain't that kind of girl, and you shouldn't be talking about others like that either."

His brows arched. "You sayin' Beverly ain't the kind of girl who'd marry a fella just from the looks of him?"

She settled her arms against her chest, "Maybe she was, but she's got a boy now. They're going steady and everything."

A hearty laugh escaped him. "How long do you think that'll last?"

"Long enough for you to get me to the diner in one piece."

They continued cruising along the highway. Trees and grassy banks lined the road between here and there. An old, abandoned gas station sat decaying on the side of the road to her right, its red painted pumps and wooden overhang were left to succumb to the elements. The radio continued to blare the next best tune across the airways.

"You gonna be working at your daddy's diner your whole life?" Billy asked.

"No. I have plans."

"What plans? The nurse thing?" Prairie eyed him coldly as he spoke. "How do you plan to pay for that?"

She squeezed her arms around her waist. "I've been saving up and working hard. Something you don't know a lick about."

Billy shook his head. "It will take you ages to make that kind of bread. Why do all that when you can just marry me, and then you won't need to worry about work?"

She crossed her arms and continued to stare out the passenger window. Billy loved to ruffle her feathers. It wasn't easy, but with him she had a particularly short fuse. Maybe it was because he never let up, and she didn't think she could ever give him what he wanted. Seemed wrong for her to keep him as a friend knowing he didn't want to be just that, but she couldn't let him go.

"You know I'm only pulling your leg," a hint of sincerity mixed with the brevity of his voice. "Come on, Prairie. I didn't mean it."

She glared at him, raising her brow, "You sure? I think you'd like me doing everything your little heart desires."

He shrugged, "Yeah, but you won't."

"Money can't buy you that from me."

His eye-catching smirk captured Prairie's full attention. "You know I don't care about all that. That's too easy."

His focus came back to the road, but she could tell he was thinking with the way those baby blues kept shifting while that smile still tickled the corners of his mouth.

"Remember the holidays two years back?" He said, "You told me you didn't want anything fancy."

Prairie looked down at her hands, unable to hide the un-abashed excitement from that rekindled memory, "You made me that scarf." She looked up, her freckled cheeks bright with joy. "Knitted it with your own hands."

"It was ugly as sin," he chuckled.

"I didn't care what it looked like."

He glanced at her, keen to keep the conversation grounded in their past. "And the concert at the park?"

There was so much about that day that was perfect. The gazebo was all lit up with white lights and tinsel. It sparkled like a star in the clear black night. The brass band played in their red coats and dark Eskimo caps, filling the air with cheer and good will to all in attendance. The night would have been unbearably cold had it not been for the bonfire and hot chocolate brewing to keep the citizens of Oak Springs warm. Sweet treats kept the atmosphere fresh with the comforts of home. The church had a donation basket to collect funds for folks who had fallen on hard times. Billy put his usual wad of cash in there, happy to give back.

For a rich boy, he was always willing to part with what his family blessed him with. He got that from his mother's good nature. Prairie had been to a number of Hemsworth fundraisers and appreciation dinners in her day, along with her folks. It was always a good time filled with merriment and giving hearts. Prairie never thought a day would come when the Hemsworth name would shift from something so wonderful to what it is now. Still a name that meant wealth and success, but the days of charity dinners were long gone, and it happened in the blink of an eye.

"I remember how sharp you looked," Prairie said, "with that green suit and red tie."

"What about you," he leaned toward her, "That long sleeved red dress and your white cardigan. Nearly knocked me out of my shoes when I saw you especially with the mistletoe in your hair. Woo," he looked at her, "don't think I'll ever forget it."

Everything that made her fall in love with him came flooding back. How he saw her, the way he admired every detail of their relationship and took care of it like nothing else mattered to him. It would be so easy to fall all over again: even after everything that happened. There was a reason she said no, but sometimes she wanted to say yes. If that Billy from the holiday party in the park proved he was still in there somewhere, then she'd say yes in a heartbeat.

The music died down and a man's voice took over the radio.

"We interrupt your regularly scheduled programming to bring you a special report. There's been another victim in the Route 43 murders. A man was found ten miles outside of Albany, moving north toward Oak Springs."

Billy moved to turn the knob, but Prairie reached out her hand to push him away. "No, keep it on!"

"The body was found in a ditch after being ripped from the window of a 1955 green and white Hudson Hornet. Other than a woman's shoes and lipstick, no weapon was found at the scene. The authorities are declaring it death by mauling."

"I'm not hearing anymore of that." Billy switched the station. The smooth voice of Buddy Holly took over as they continued toward the diner.

Prairie folded her hands in her lap while her heart skipped a few beats. Another killing, done the same way as the rest. The police were sure it was a creature, some bear gone over the edge. No man would do that. How could they?

The drifter and his bloody arm stood out like a sore thumb in her mind. She tried to remember what it looked like. Small beads of blood had mixed with the rain, as if it was coming from multiple cuts and not just one, the way someone might look after going through a window.

They drove past the scenic picnic area, the last landmark on the highway before reaching the diner. "It's just a wolf or something." Billy said, seeing her face drawn in thought.

Prairie folded her arms across her chest to stop her mind from spinning, "A wolf pulling men out of their cars? That doesn't make a heap of sense."

"Even so, it's not something you need to worry about."

"And what's with them finding all these ladies' things in the cars but no lady. Don't you think that's a bit funny?"

"Geez, Prairie." Billy shifted in the driver's seat. "You ain't no officer of the law. You're a waitress." He glanced at her. "So, stick to what you know, and stop being so damn curious all the time."

Prairie's mouth twisted as she fell back against the seat. She couldn't help being curious. Asking questions came naturally to her ever since she was in pigtails. She poured over books from Carolyn Keene and Agatha Christie, spending many a rainy night under her covers with a flashlight, wondering what clues would be revealed with a single turn of a page. Her mama always said reading those stories would get her into trouble one day.

They turned onto the long front lot of the diner. *Moonlight* flashed its attractive red and white lights, inviting weary travelers to partake in warm coffee and feel-good eats. Billy pulled up into a spot, stepping out of the car with one smooth swing. With a deep breath, Prairie adjusted her blue and white uniform, and fixed the tie holding her hair back. Billy grabbed at the door handle and waited for her to step out.

"So, what are you up to tonight?" Prairie asked as she got out of the car.

"My uncle's got me doing some things."

Prairie cringed. She never liked Billy's uncle. He was blunt and unfeeling. An up-to-no-good scoundrel if she ever saw one. If she learned anything from the mysteries she'd read, it was to stay away from men like him.

They walked up to the door, which Billy opened for her as well. A proper gentleman when he wanted to be.

"He's showing me the ropes. I oversaw a department store shipment just the other day. No sweat. When I finally take over the business, I'll know exactly what to do."

They walked into the diner. A woman with curly brown hair and faded freckles across her button-nosed face smiled up at them warmly. "There's my girl."

"Hi, Mama." Prairie walked up to her mother and gave her a peck on the cheek.

"Mrs. O'Shea. Good afternoon." Billy smiled as he came up behind Prairie.

"My, my, my. Billy Hemsworth. Still carting my daughter around every chance you get? And it's Lorna, for the hundredth time."

"Billy." A tall, long-faced fellow came lumbering up toward the counter. He had on a white button-down shirt and dark slacks. An apron was slung around his waist. His eyes were drawn and prominent bags hung like laundry on a line beneath them. "Good to see you. How have you been?" His dull Irish accent was almost unrecognizable, a result of living the American dream.

"Just swell, Mr. O'Shea."

"For god's sakes, call me Jerry. I've known you since you were a boy." He patted Billy on the shoulder. "No need to be so formal."

"There is when your daughter is involved."

Lorna dusted off some crumbs from Jerry's shirt before planting her hand on his chest.

"Well, I best be off now." Billy looked at Prairie, "You need me to come get you in the morning?"

"Bev will take me home." Her parents looked at her expectedly as she tried to shy away from him. "Thanks for the lift."

"Anytime. Have a good night."

Both Jerry and Lorna waved their goodbye to the Hemsworth heir. Closing her eyes, Prairie took a deep breath before turning on her heels to punch her timecard.

"Prairie." Her dad's voice stopped her. He came around and stood beside her. "Elliot told us about the colored fella that came in here this morning."

"What about him?" She tried to sound sure of herself. She did nothing wrong. Not many colored folk came through here, but it wasn't uncommon.

"Elliot said he looked like he was up to no good."

"Elliot will say that about anyone who doesn't look like him." Prairie sighed. "He was a paying customer. You told me not to turn down anybody who can drop a dime in this place."

"And I meant it. Every color is welcome in this diner, as long as they got dough in their pocket. We need all the business we can get, but that doesn't mean you shouldn't be careful. With all the killings going on around here, you can't be too sure of people."

"He wasn't doing anything wrong. He just wanted some coffee and he left."

Lorna came up behind her, placing her hands comfortingly on her daughter's arms, "We know how you are with people, always willing to talk and stretch a hand." Prairie fell on her mother's concerned gaze. "Just be more careful with who you're offering it to."

It was understandable; her parents wanted her to be safe with everything that was going on. Prairie nodded willingly, knowing her folks would only take her side and no one else's. "I'll be more careful."

"That's my girl." Lorna gave her a kiss on the side of her head. "Now, wash up. Those tables aren't going to serve themselves!"

Chapter 3
The Detective

Another early morning of the usual truckers and the occasional munchers left a lot to be desired in the diner. Prairie wiped down the counters for the hundredth time since 1 a.m. Nobody was coming the rest of the morning until the sun came up. Beverly was staring at herself in her powder mirror pursing her lips and angling her head to see which way she looked best.

"You know you're a heart stopper, Bev." Prairie smiled as she nudged Beverly's shoulder. "What do you have to worry about?"

Beverly smirked. "Just keeping up appearances is all. In case somebody worth my eye decides to stroll in here."

"What about Georgie?" Prairie asked. "You were talking my ear off the other day about him."

"He's still around." Bev snapped her powder closed. "But you never know."

Rolling her eyes, Prairie pushed through the swinging doors into the kitchen. Elliot was leaning against the corner of the stove, his nose shoved in yesterday morning's paper. A smoke stick hung out of the side of his mouth. He looked up as she entered and made her way to the plates to bring some up front.

"You read about this other murder?" he asked.

Chills ran up her spine. She didn't want to think that the per-

son killing all the men along the highway was still out there. "I heard about it on the radio on the way here."

"Folks think it's an animal." He sniffed while turning the page. "Can't say I believe that." He eyed Prairie as she came back to the door. "Reckon your drifter had something to do with it."

She pursed her lips, giving him a look that would take the paint off a quick ride. "What you saying *my* drifter for?"

"Just sayin'."

Prairie leaned the plates on her hip. "And I don't appreciate you mouthing off to my daddy about that either. We ain't kids here, Elliot."

"I was concerned, is all." He pushed his glasses up the bridge of his nose. "A girl like you shouldn't be talking to a spook." His gaze returned to the paper. "Just not right."

"You're not right, Elliot." Prairie pushed against the door. "Leave me out of your minding or I'll get Wanda to switch you for overstepping where you don't need to overstep."

Back behind the counter, Prairie walked to the right to stash the plates, but when she looked up, she saw a man in a fedora and brown trench coat standing on the other side of the counter, across from Beverly. Bev turned on her heels. Her eyes were swimming with concern.

"Prairie." She spoke calmly, despite her fingers fidgeting against the counter. "This man would like to speak to you."

The man peeled away from the counter and fished in the inside pocket of his jacket, pulling out a badge and flashing it for her to see. "Good morning, miss. My name is Detective Greenway."

"Oh." Prairie looked from Beverly and back to the detective. "Good morning to you too, Detective." She slid the plates onto the counter. Pressing her apron, she walked over to where he stood, and kept her eyes focused. "What can I help you with?"

Greenway had an almost smokey look about him. His dark

hair was barely visible under his cap. His five o'clock shadow complimented his strong jaw and deep, down-turned eyes. He wasn't that much taller than her, but he carried himself like he could overshadow anyone who stood toe to toe with him.

He tucked his badge back in his trench coat pocket. "I'm investigating the Route 43 murders as you've probably deduced."

"Yes, I . . . suppose that would be your reason for coming here."

"We had a tip on a drifter coming through between here and Albany. A colored man about six feet tall. Scar on the left side of his face. Seen anyone that fits that description recently?"

Beverly curled her lips inward. She had more than likely already told him about the drifter that came in here the other night. Prairie was in no position to lie, especially when people's lives were in danger.

"Yes, as a matter of fact, there was a man who came here yesterday morning." Prairie gestured toward a stool at the counter not too far from the detective. "Sat right there. Ordered a black coffee."

Greenway glanced at the stool, scribbling words in his pad of paper. "Did he do or say anything?"

She shrugged. "Nothing that would raise any suspicion if that's what you're asking."

"Did he say where he was headed?"

"No."

"And has he been here before?"

"Not while I've been here."

The sound of his scribbling pen grew. "And you got a good look at him?"

Prairie swallowed. She remembered his cool, slick demeanor and smooth grin. It was something she couldn't forget. For as little as he said, he sure left an impression on her. "I waited on him, so I saw him as well as I'm seeing you."

Greenway looked up from his writing. "Anything out of the ordinary that stood out to you?"

"Aside from his scar, can't say there was anything. He was soaked from the rain, but nothing else."

He looked at Beverly. "Do you often wait on colored people here?"

"The owners let anyone who pays dine here. We don't get many, but when they do come, they're always waited on just like anybody else."

He wrote more on his pad. Prairie and Beverly watched, waiting in silent anticipation for him to ask his next question.

After dotting an *I* or crossing a *T*, he smiled. "Thank you, ladies. You've been mighty kind and cooperative." He flipped the pages down, pulled out a rectangle-shaped card, and placed it on the counter. "If you see him again, give me a call."

"Of course." Beverly took the card from him.

"Regular patrols will be made every hour along the highway, so don't be alarmed if you notice a lot of police activity from here on out." Tucking his pad away, he tipped his hat to them. "You have a good morning now." He said, as he turned on his heels. The detective's coat trailed behind him as he pushed against the door and waded out into the night. Both Prairie and Beverly waited until he was in his car and peeled away from the diner before either spoke.

"Prairie." Bev turned to her. "You didn't say anything about the blood."

"And you didn't either." She reached back for the plates and scooped them against her, making her way to the shelf to house them. "He didn't ask, so why say a word?"

"Because he's the law, that's why." Bev got close to her to prevent Elliot from hearing a word of it. "Why didn't you say anything?"

"Same reason you didn't." Prairie finished up her task and

turned toward her friend. "That man was just a man passing through. He wasn't anything else. And I'd be pointing suspicions at someone who'd be made number one in the books just because he's not a white man."

Beverly sighed as her hands clasped her hips. "You sure that's the only reason?"

Prairie's head shifted back. "I'm not sure what you mean."

"Oh, come on, Prairie." Bev smirked.

"That's crazy talk, Bev."

She leaned against the counter, grabbing a cloth from her apron. "He was handsome. Like if James Dean was colored. Cool, tough and drenched from the rain." Her gaze drifted as if she was picturing him in her mind.

"Nothing wrong with looking."

Prairie lightly whipped the cloth across Beverly's arm.

"You've got your mind in the gutter at all hours of the day and night." Beverly gave a slight giggle.

"Besides, if he's like all the rest of them drifters, he won't be back here again."

"I hope you're right." Bev sighed. "I don't want the police all over this place. For your folk's sake."

Prairie placed her hands on the counter. "Best not let Elliot know about this, or we'll never hear the end of it."

"I won't tell that square anything. But if that drifter comes here again, Prairie . . . I can't promise you anything. Especially if the murders keep happening."

"Of course." Prairie nodded. "I'm with you on that." And she was. She could assume all she wanted by forcing pieces together, but who knows if they'd fit.

That drifter could have just been someone passing through who cut his arm. It could be just that. Nothing at all to do with the murders. Prairie needed to forget about it and move on, no matter how much it stuck with her. Once all this was over, it would just be a memory she'd not too soon forget. As much as that was true, she hoped he'd skipped town, if only to keep him out of the headlights of the law.

Chapter 4
The Dream

Both Lorna and Jerry walked straight into the office before Prairie could get in a word with them. The morning shift was starting to trail in, giving Bev and Prairie a call to leave, but not before she told them about the detective.

Leaning through the doorway, she watched her parents pour over the desk stacked with papers and orders for the diner. The office was small, with a square window at the corner of the room. Filing cabinets and a few snapshots of the family on summer vacation decorated the cleanly wiped wall by the punch clock and timecards at the door.

Prairie fished hers out, slid it into the top, and pulled the lever. "Daddy?" Both of her parents looked up at her as she turned to them, placing her card back in her slot. "I gotta tell you something."

"Of course, sugar pie." Jerry sighed, gesturing toward the seat in front of the desk. "Sit down."

Prairie slid between the metal arms of the chair and her hands fell into her lap. "A detective was here this morning." She reached into her apron pocket and took out his card before placing it on the desk. "He was here about the murders."

"Oh, I see." Jerry took the card and replaced his specs. "Did he ask anything specific?"

She shook her head. "No. Just if we've seen anyone suspicious, is all."

"Jerry." Lorna cut in. "Maybe you should take over the early morning shift. With these killings, I don't want Prairie and Bev being here all night alone."

"They got Elliot." Jerry slipped the card in his carousel.

"We're fine, mama. I can take care of myself."

Lorna looked at her daughter. "I know you can, Prairie. But whoever is doing this is rattling a lot of cages. I just want you to be safe."

"Police will be all over the highway day and night, I'm sure, and we got the detective's number now." Jerry sniffed, getting back to the paperwork on the desk. "They'll probably catch the goon good. Sooner or later."

"Who's taking you home this morning?" Lorna asked.

"Oh, Bev is." Prairie hesitated to move, the same nagging question she'd been asking her folks for months still ragging on her mind. They always said the same thing, and judging by the numbers she saw on the bills, she didn't think their tune would change.

"I wanted to ask about . . . nursing school."

Both Jerry and Lorna stopped what they were doing to focus on her. "Prairie." Jerry took off his specs. "We've been over this."

"I know, Daddy, but I got some saved up for it. And the program over at the hospital in Albany is opening up again soon for new students."

"Prairie." Lorna sighed. "I know how much you want this. And we wish we could give you the money to do that, but . . ." she looked down at the papers. "The diner's still not doing as well as we'd like it to. We could use your help here. For a little longer."

"How much longer?"

"For as long as you'll stay." Jerry sighed. "Look, sugar, I know it's not the answer you want to hear. With all them murders happening, the diner's suffering for it. Maybe . . . when all this blows over, your Ma and I can give you the rest of the money. A few more months. Can you give us that?"

Prairie watched them, wishing she had the heart to say no. She loved her folks, more than anything in this world, but nursing was her calling. She knew ever since she was a little girl when her father would tell her stories about the war. She wanted to help all the wounded and broken souls, and even though the war was over, the call was still there.

"Of course, Daddy." Prairie forced a smile. Jerry reached over and took her chin between his fingers.

"That's my girl."

She rose from the seat and headed from the office. Lorna put a hand on her shoulder as she passed the desk. "Love you."

"Love you too, mama."

She slipped through the kitchen and moved toward the swinging doors. Just as she was about to pass through them, another body stopped short to keep from running into her. Prairie stepped back.

"Excuse me, I didn't see you coming."

The man was tall and stocky, with light pepper-brown hair. A speckled sport coat and dark brown slacks donned his image, and a nicely pressed tie sat against the clean curve of his shirt.

"No need to worry." He said with a grin. "You're Jerry's girl, aren't you?"

"Yes. I . . . Mr. Hemsworth." Prairie shook her head. "I'm sorry, I didn't recognize you."

Bernard Hemsworth. Billy's uncle. Now that she recognized him, her stomach got all queasy. There was something about him that didn't sit right with her. Maybe because he was the opposite of Billy's parents, Desmond and Mary, who were such a fun-loving pair. Her folks and them had been keepers since after the war. But Bernard was hard and shifty, even when he painted that likable smirk on his face.

After a car accident took Billy's parents, things weren't the same between the families. Though Bernard would visit from time to time.

"Billy talks a lot about you." He said. "If he focused on his work more than girls, I'd have nothing to worry about."

Prairie bit her lip. "Billy's got a lot going for him, Mr. Hemsworth. He'd do his father proud if you offered him the chance."

He smirked. "Is that you telling me or him telling you to tell me?"

She straightened her posture. "I speak for nobody but myself."

"That so?" Bernard dove into his inside pocket and pulled out a pack of smokes, slipping one between his lips. "No wonder Billy likes you so much."

"Bernard." Jerry snuck around her and offered him his hand. "Good of you to stop by."

"Of course, Jerry." Bernard shook his hand. "Always a pleasure to see you. Have you thought about my offer?"

Jerry's lips tightened, like someone pulling a close line taught between two trees. "Let's keep the business talk in the office, if you don't mind, Bernard."

"Course." Bernard's gaze fell to Prairie. "Nice to see you again."

"Likewise, Mr. Hemsworth." Prairie said.

Jerry ushered the businessman into his office. Flexing her fingers, she passed through the doors and onto the main floor.

What offer was that sly fox talking about?

Prairie knew the diner had been hit hard since the murders started. Even before then, they were never swimming in dough. Could it really be that bad?

Beverly was leaning against the shiny aluminum wall with Georgie's jacket draped over her shoulders.

"What took you so long?"

They went out into the parking lot, past the tall standing sign of the Moonlight Diner. Walking up to her pink Dodge, Prairie couldn't get the heavy words between Bernard and her Daddy out of her mind.

Bev popped some Bazooka as she slid on her white cat shades. "What's eating you?"

Her eyes shot to her friend. "Oh, nothing. Just something Daddy was sayin' that's all."

Bev wasn't too keen to stay on the subject. "You're not working next Thursday night, are you?"

Prairie shook her head. "No. Why do you ask?"

"There's that movie I've been wanting to see at the drive-in. Georgie ain't too keen on going. If you want to tag along."

"I'd welcome that." They both opened the car doors and sat inside. "And I don't believe you when you say Georgie ain't keen on going. A chance to neck in the car doesn't seem like something he'd want to say no to."

Beverly smirked. "Maybe he needs a break, is all." She put the key in the ignition. "Can't say I blame him. It's hard keeping' up with me."

Rolling her eyes, Prairie smiled as they pulled out. She was happy to think on something else other than the delay of her dream of becoming a nurse, her father's dealings with Bernard Hemsworth, the murders, Billy's constant nagging, and that lonely drifter.

Chapter 5
The Thunderbird

It had been close to a week since Detective Greenway came to question her about the drifter, and all was quiet. No other murders happened either, a clear sign that things had died down enough to breathe.

The ride to the diner was quiet. Billy wasn't his usual, forward self. Prairie watched him; his knuckles were almost ghost white from gripping the wheel so hard. The pulse on the side of his neck visibly beat like a drum. She wanted to say something but couldn't think of the right words.

Today was his mother's birthday.

She remembered when she was little, when both their daddies were drafted during the war, and her and her mama would go to the Hemsworth house to celebrate. Prairie always loved that her birthday was so close to his mother's because they would always have a joint party. But it was never really for Mary.

The parties always had balloons of all colors and sizes. The Hemsworths had a giant swimming pool with a diving board and a water polo net. One year, there was a whole mini circus with a petting zoo and pony rides. A band played their favorite songs, and the cake was always so tall that Prairie could stand inside it if she wanted to.

Mary always said Prairie was the daughter she never had.

"What's on your mind, Billy?" she asked, hoping to jog him out of this funk he was in.

Billy glanced at her, but only for a quick minute, "Nothing."

She sighed, hoping what she was about to say wouldn't rattle him up, "I miss her too. Both of them."

He puckered his lips, twisting them around like he was trying to keep himself from saying something. Aside from a nod, he didn't say anything. Just kept on driving.

"It's not good to keep all that inside," she added, moving her hand to rest on the inside of his arm. "You know you can talk to me."

"I know that," he pulled himself away and gripped the wheel lower to keep her off him.

Prairie rubbed her tongue over her teeth. There was only so much she could say to him. If he wanted to talk, he would have to make the effort. When it first happened, he was with her every day. At her home, sleeping on the couch, pouring himself out to her almost every night for two solid weeks. When they held the funeral, he didn't cry, not a single tear. And he hadn't since. Breathing a word of it was worse than a curse to him. Even on the first anniversary of their death, he seemed like he was running from it.

Prairie was sure Bernard had got to him, somehow convincing him that his grief was a weakness. Even more reason to keep that man as far away from her and her family as possible.

With a deep sigh, Billy looked at her, his chin low, "I don't want to talk about it, Prairie."

"Well, what if I want to talk about it?"

"I don't want to hear it," he said. "What I wanna talk about is us."

Prairie crossed her arms and leaned back into the seat, "What do you mean by *us*?"

"How much longer we gonna be playing this game, Prairie?" Billy gripped the wheel, his tongue flicking out to moisten his lips.

"I don't know what game you're talking about."

The Bel Air soared across the highway with a gentle hum. Prairie leaned on the door, peering out the window at the rushing green of the trees on their way to the Moonlight Diner.

"Me being your personal driver is what I'm saying." Billy huffed. "You think I do this for every girl that glances my way?"

Prairie shook her head. "Billy, I've known you since we were picking our noses and throwing dirt at Mr. Fuller's mean old mutt." She glanced at him and caught his eye. "I'm not just any girl to you, and you're not just any boy to me."

"So, what am I then?" A strand of slicked hair fell against his forehead.

Prairie eyed him cooly, but she already knew what he wanted to hear. Billy could get any girl he wanted with one flash of his teeth and his green gold waving in their faces. Being a Hemsworth had luxuries any girl would fancy having for herself. Money bought a lot of things, even love. But Billy knew he couldn't buy her love, and that made him all the more keen to earn it. No matter how many times she turned him down.

"I'm your friend, Billy." She mouthed. "Probably the only real one you got. And if you think I'm anything but that, you don't need to take me to work anymore. You don't even got to talk to me if you don't want to."

Cutting the wheel to the right, Billy skidded the car to a halt on the side of the road. A dirt cloud sprung up over the windshield, slowly billowing into the cracks of the windows.

"What are you doing?" She protested, her curls snapping across the back of her neck as she turned to look at him.

With an upturned scowl, Billy combed his fingers through his hair, releasing more strands into his face. "You get me so frosted it stings, Prairie."

She sighed, coming off the car door. "Billy, we've danced this dance before. It never works out."

"I can make it work. I know I can."

She shook her head. "You can't just make yourself like somebody like that."

"Come on, Prairie." Billy leaned into her seat. "You did once. Maybe you still do, and you don't know it yet."

She pressed her lips, his closeness both making her skin crawl and pattering her heart something terrible. Billy was a dreamboat, and he knew her better than anyone. She'd be crazy not to think they'd be made in the shade. She knew how to handle his brashness and he knew how to handle hers. They were like peas and carrots before, but there was always something missing. Something no amount of knowing could help bake into what love was supposed to be.

She settled back against the car door, trying not to be lured by his Paul Newman eyes. "I know what I see, Billy."

"Look," He inched closer. "I know I can be a lot. I . . . just got a lot going on."

"That you won't talk to me about," she huffed, "when did I become someone you can't talk to?"

He looked down, weighing his words with his hand on the back of her headrest, "I can't, I just..."

She looked away, biting her tongue as her chest rose and fell with steady urgency. Every time this came up, it got harder and harder to see it coming out okay. The distance he put between them hurt more than anything. Maybe that's why she couldn't say yes, because how could she be with someone who couldn't trust her to understand what he was going through. "Billy—"

He reached for her face and, like a jack rabbit, pulled her toward him to try and steal a kiss. Just before he could get his meat hooks in her any deeper, Prairie shoved him back and flipped the handle, shooting out the door onto the side of the road.

"I can't believe you, Billy!" She shouted as she stormed in front, making her way down the road.

Billy slammed the door as he skidded around the car, his loafers kicking up sand as he grabbed her arm. "Where you going?"

She spun to face him. "I'm going to work." She glared as she pulled herself free and continued walking.

"You gonna walk? You're off your rocker." He took her again, this time holding firmly at the crux of her arm. Billy whipped her around as Prairie's hands stopped her from crashing against his chest, pushing against him.

"Let go of me."

Billy eased off but didn't let go. He squinted, like he was trying to shake off this side of him that was coming out, the side Prairie wished he never adopted to begin with.

"Come on, Prairie," he sighed, "I just . . . I don't wanna fight with you."

"You'd rather me tell you what you wanna hear, is that it? To make you feel better?"

She jerked at his hold, barely slipping away, "You don't get what you want by treating people this way, especially someone you claim to *love* so much." She got up on her toes to look him square in the eye. Red flooded his face, tightening his jaw at the words he didn't want to hear spilling from her mouth, "So, until you mind your attitude, my answer is no. No. No. No. And no!"

"God damn it, Prairie." his finger tightened, locking her in good.

"Let go of me, William Hemsworth. I ain't gonna ask you again."

"Or what?" His mouth tightened. "Nobody yanks my chain like you do, Prairie. I'm tired of you saying no."

"Get used to it, cuz I'm not ever saying yes to you again!"

In that split moment, a midnight Thunderbird roared past them, its tires slid from the road onto the dirt a few feet from their car. Both Prairie and Billy watched as the dark chariot's engine cut. The driver's side door swung open. Prairie's gaze watched as the keen drifter from a week before rose above the roof, collar popped and boots crunching in the dirt.

Chapter 6
The Ride

He walked toward them with his hands in his jean pockets, a lit Camel stick hanging from his mouth. He planted himself firmly, legs shoulder-width apart and head held high.

"Best take your hands off the lady." He spoke low but stern. Prairie could feel the hair on her arms stand on end.

Billy yanked Prairie aside, taking a few steps forward. "Get out of here, negro. This ain't your business."

The drifter slowly plucked the stick from his mouth and dropped it to the ground. His boots snuffed it into the dirt. "I can make it my business."

The grip on her arm loosened. Billy swallowed harshly, weighing what he should do next.

As he stewed, Prairie ripped herself from him, cradling her arm to her chest as she skirted away. Her sudden absence shifted Billy's attention and he reached for her. "Where you going?" She jumped away, and he called out, "Get back here, Prairie."

"I'm not going anywhere with you!" Her feet brought her closer to the drifter.

The drifter took a step in front of her. His expression was cool and focused on Billy, watching his every move. "You okay, ma'am?"

"I'm fine." Prairie breathed.

"Going somewhere?" His dark face glanced back to her, soft brown eyes catching the air in her throat.

"Yes, I'm headed to work."

"You ain't going with this spook, Prairie!"

She glared at Billy. "I'd rather ride with him than go anywhere with you!" Before she had time to change her mind, she sprinted toward the drifter's ride, opened the passenger side door and slid into the seat.

"Prairie—" Billy's voice cut out as she slammed the door, strapped on the belt, and settled down in the leather. "Prairie!" Billy took a step forward before focusing on the drifter blocking his way. His chin tensed as he stood, mouth agape, not sure what to do. So, he did what he did best. With fists clenched and teeth gnashed, Billy turned back toward his Bel Air and got inside. The drifter didn't move an inch as he watched Billy handle the wheel before he peeled away on to the open road.

Once the dust settled, the drifter turned toward the car. He slowly walked around the back and went into the driver's seat. He closed the door gently and let the silence creep in as a slow exhale drew from his nostrils.

"Where to, ma'am?"

Prairie pushed her frazzled mahogany hair behind her ears, nerves shooting through her fingers as she flashed her green eyes to him. "Moonlight Diner. If you don't mind?"

"Not at all, miss." He turned the key in the ignition and the engine purred to life. "Not at all."

The drifter kept his eyes on the road with one hand gripping the smooth wheel as Johnny Cash pounded on the radio. Prairie's eyes were forward, not wanting to appear rude by searching all over his car to find out more clues about him. Ma always said you can tell a lot about a man by how he keeps his car. From the outside, it seemed very well taken care of. The clean leather seats looked like they had never carried a hint of dirt on them their entire life; and the car didn't smell too heavy of cigarette smoke. It was clear it meant something to him unless there was another reason he was keeping up appearances.

"Any man who puts his hands on a woman ain't no man."

Her attention shifted from the cleanliness of the car to him. She shook her head. "Billy's not always that bad. He just . . . I don't know."

He didn't look at her and kept his eyes on the road. "Sure looked bad to me."

Prairie tightened her arms in her lap, "It wasn't anything I couldn't handle."

"Then why'd you get in my car?"

Sharp eyes stung in his direction, "Because you offered."

The drifter squeezed the wheel with his brawny hands, "You take rides from colored folk often then?"

"No, I . . ." he glanced at her, and her pulse quickened. Prairie turned back around and stared at the white lines peppering the road ahead of them, "I don't see how that's any of your business."

She looked at the apron of her uniform and pulled at the ends to stifle the unusual mix of flustered emotions he was driving out of her. She wanted to defend herself, and Billy, crazy enough. She knew he was wrong for what he did, but it was hard to be strong sitting in this stranger's car. She did not know this man, nor what he did. Not even if he did anything at all. He was an utter mystery her curiosity yearned to solve. So much that, if he was the killer, it didn't stop her from inviting herself into his space.

But if he did kill those people, why did I get in?

"You could have just passed us by," she said, not wanting to see the expression on his face, "like most anyone else would have."

The low vocals from the radio and gentle hum of the car engine filled the silence. Prairie took a long breath and plucked up the courage to look his way. He was still sitting there, jaw locked, with a smoke stick between his fingers at the wheel.

"Why did you stop, anyway?"

His soft brown eyes looked at her as the corner of his mouth drew up in a mock sneer before parting from his words, "Because it was the right thing to do."

After keeping on his eyes for more than she should have, she returned to her silent vigil of the highway.

The right thing to do, that's the answer any self-respecting gentlemen would give.

Maybe he was just that: a gentleman. If she hadn't already thought he had something to do with those murders, it would have felt like a more true answer. Murderers didn't do the right thing, did they? No, they did what was wrong: never what was right.

Prairie looked behind her at the bench. The car looked immaculately clean there too. The leather seats were polished without a crumb to their name. A few burlap bags and a torchlight sat on the corner of the bench. Looking at the drifter, she shifted uncomfortably in her seat, sandwiching her hands between her knees.

"How's your arm?"

He didn't bother to look at her. "It's better now."

She smoothed out her blue and white uniform, feeling the light layer of nervous sweat coat the cotton, "You hear about those killings?"

"Sure have."

"A detective came to the diner." She looked back at him, trying not to let her uneasiness show. "He asked about you."

His lips pressed for a drop. "What'd ya tell him?"

"Just that you came in, had coffee, and left."

"You ain't say nothing about my arm?"

Prairie went lip-tight. Why was she even telling this to him? She was silently taking sides when she had no business in this man's affairs at all. It was all too tempting, this entire happenstance. A chance at her own Nancy Drew story. Even if she didn't think he'd killed those men, just the idea that maybe he did was enough to keep herself wanting. It would have been easier to just come out and ask if he killed them or not, but learning that her assumptions of his character were wrong kept it from spilling out.

"No." She swallowed, reaching to grasp her resting arm. "I didn't think he needed to know anything about that."

His dark eyes watched her like he was trying to answer for her. "Why's that?"

Prairie could tell him the same thing she told Beverly, but it didn't make sense to bring up her stance on society and how it treated those who were different. The real reason was troubling to her. Anyone confronted by a badge wouldn't hide a thing for a stranger. He didn't know her, and she didn't know him from a hole in the wall. But she couldn't come clean, and she didn't quite know why.

"You're not the killer."

His brow raised. "How do you know I'm not?"

Ants crawled up and down her arms. She allowed herself to really look at him. It wasn't easy seeing what was under people's skin. Some didn't bother to hide it, like Billy's uncle, but others were keen to keep it locked away. This drifter sure was trying, but despite his defensiveness, there was something most wouldn't be patient enough to see in those big brown windows to his soul.

"Your eyes, I suppose. They aren't a killer's eyes."

The car engine and muffled tunes couldn't drown out the tension. Prairie watched his gaze shift to observe her from top to bottom. She couldn't imagine what he was thinking; but she wasn't just saying it to be nice. It's what she believed after getting to look at him properly. Through all the back and forth that was going on inside the cab, there was one thing Prairie wasn't feeling while she sat in the passenger's seat.

She wasn't afraid.

A white Irish-bred girl with freckles complimenting a colored man on his eyes wasn't proper, but honesty ran in her blood, and she couldn't help but appreciate those honey-soaked browns of his.

Perhaps she'd overstepped.

"You ever see a killer's eyes before?"

His question pulled her back to the seat and out of his gaze. "Can't say I have."

"Then how would you know what they look like?"

She shrugged, nerves getting the better of her. "I suppose I don't. It was just a feeling." She tucked her chin, looking down. "I guess you very well could be."

A sweet, hearty laugh shook his entire body, breaking the tension as he burst from the seams. "You sure are nosey for a waitress, Miss. Prairie."

Prairie shook away the unsettledness with a relieved smile. "You don't have to call me Miss. Just Prairie is fine."

"I apologize." He looked at her again. "Prairie."

Him saying her name made the hair on her arms stand on end. The air between them was lighter, but for some reason, she couldn't quite steady her breath.

It wasn't long before they reached the diner. The drifter pulled the car right up to the door, shifting to park while the engine still purred with life. Prairie didn't move, even though she knew her shift was starting soon. The sun had already begun to kiss the tops of the trees goodnight as it left a deep amber glaze across the whisking clouds above.

"You never did tell me your name."

That grin captured her again as she watched his hard demeanor change to one of genuine curiosity. "What you be needin' my name for?"

"To thank you properly."

He leaned against the door, his hand coming off the wheel. "My name is Marrok."

"Marrok." She repeated softly. "That's an original name." They stayed quiet, watching the other without suggesting they part.

Prairie undid the belt from her waist with a sigh. "Well, Marrok, thank you for the ride." She opened the door and stepped out, lingering between the door and the seat to keep her green eyes on his honey browns.

"Anytime, Prairie." A smile painted across his face, creasing his scar against the corners of his eyes.

"You be safe now." She closed the door, hearing it meet the frame, and stepped back toward the diner.

The car rolled through the parking lot. Prairie watched as Marrok lifted his hand to her before the tires met the road. Standing in the wake of the diner, she didn't realize how much her heart was pattering against her ribs until she had a minute to collect herself. She brought her hand to her chest and rubbed her palm gently over her name sewn into her uniform. Taking a deep breath, she turned tail into the diner.

Chapter 7
The Drive-In

Concession characters danced on the big screen of the dirt lot at the drive-in. Beverly was still gussying up her hair and makeup in the driver's seat. The windows were open, letting the cool summer air tickle the backs of their necks every time it decided to blow by.

"What are you making yourself up for?" Prairie smirked, admiring her friend's luscious curls and perfect brown eyes. "Who are you trying to impress?"

"A girl should always look her best." Bev shut her cosmetics case and placed it back inside her purse. "I could do yours if you want."

Prairie trained her focus back on the dancing hot dogs and popcorn boxes. "I don't need any of that."

"Oh, come on, Prairie." Bev smirked. "You tellin' me you wouldn't want to catch the eye of some fella in this lot? I'm sure there are plenty of available men just waiting to sweep you off your feet."

"Maybe I don't wanna be swept off my feet." She leaned her elbow on the car door with a huff. "I got my hands full trying to keep Billy at bay anyway."

Bev settled back in her seat. "I don't know why you don't ride

with him. He's crazy about you, Prairie. It's not nice dragging him along like you're gonna change your mind."

"I don't need anybody crazy about me. Especially with him acting the way he does." She glanced at Bev.

"What do you mean?"

Prairie hesitated. She hadn't told anybody about Billy trying to steal a kiss from her and Marrok riding in like a gallant cowboy to carry her away in his Thunderbird. Holding her breath, she sat up in the seat.

"Billy tried to kiss me the other day. When he was taking me to work."

"Without you asking him to?" Bev turned completely toward her. "Why didn't you tell me?"

"Cuz I got . . . picked up . . . by somebody."

"Who?"

Her fingers fiddled on the edge of her blue striped skirt. "That drifter."

Bev's eyes grew wide. "Prairie O'Shea." She breathed. "You telling me that drifter came and *dropped* Billy?"

She shook her head. "Nobody dropped anybody! I was trying to get away from Billy and he drove up and said he'd give me a ride. Billy was yanking at me to get back in the car."

"That's the most gallant thing I ever heard. But the stupidest thing for you." Beverly glanced at the screen, as the beginning credits of "Another Time, Another Place" came through. "You don't know that man, Prairie, and the cops are looking at him for those murders." She leaned toward her. "He could have killed you!"

"But he didn't cuz I'm sitting with you now." Her gaze met the screen as Sean Connery's distinguished voice coated her ears.

"You talk to him?"

"Of course, I talked to him."

Bev took her arm. "Look, Prairie. I'm all for getting lost in a man's eyes. But you gotta be careful. People will pick you out like a sore thumb for being all dreamy about a negro. Especially with them killings popping up all over 43."

Prairie tucked her locks behind her ear. It was foolish of her to do that. Foolish and dangerous. Her parents warned her to be careful and she deliberately disobeyed them, all because she was so keen on wanting to know more. She wasn't even careful in their conversation, spilling out every little scrap to him like she had an obligation to. She acted loose. Saying it was because of one thing over another just tied her up even more. That look, that deep soulful look in his eyes . . . made her want like never before.

Even so, there was no question that she acted carelessly, and she couldn't do that. Not now.

She grasped Bev's hand and squeezed it with a smile. "I know, Bev. I'm being careful."

"Good." With a returning smile, Bev let go of her arm. "Now, let's get lost in another looker." She let loose a breath. "Connery can knock on my door any day of the week."

They started watching the movie and concentrated on the story—reacting as any girl swooning over a love triangle would. It wasn't too much longer before Prairie started to feel parched. Looking over to Bev, she nudged her friend gingerly. "Want anything from the stand? I'm buying."

"Share some popcorn with me? And grab me a soda too."

"All right, I'll be right back." She grabbed her change purse and opened the door before stepping onto the lot of cars. She walked toward the concession stand in the back where there were a few seated patrons watching from the offered chairs just in front. They laughed and snickered while dropping JuJu's and caramel corn into their mouths.

She got in line, which wasn't too long since the movie had just started, and most people already had what they needed to hold them over for the next hour. On the far side of the lot was another stand with a line coiled in front of it like a snake. The drive-in had a colored area in the back with their own spot to grab refreshments. It seemed less efficient and maybe even neglected. It was strange how these divides were always there, part of the scenery, yet it wasn't until now that she noticed them with a subtle sense of unfairness.

Prairie held on to the railing and glanced out over the open lot behind the concession building. There was a small playground with swings and a teeter-totter looking lonely in the waning moonlight. A red and white shed sat next to one of the metal slides. That was probably where the groundskeeper kept all the equipment needed to keep this place tidy after a night of movies.

Just before she moved up the line, there was a hint of movement from the edge of the shed. It flashed and then disappeared again. Kicked dirt plumed out from behind the shed from whatever disturbed it. Tapping her Kerrybrooke flats, Prairie moved against the rail and slipped out between the gap. It was probably nothing but a stray dog or something. What if it was hurt? She couldn't just sit by and not try to help.

As she inched closer, she smoothed her swing skirt against her legs and adjusted her blouse as she gazed back toward the now retreating safety of the drive-in. A stifled grunt stopped her in her tracks. With a gentle swallow, Prairie carefully approached. She gave herself a wide berth, coming around the slide to get a better view of what was going on.

When her eyes finally crested the corner, she skidded to a halt. A bald, stout man was being held by the collar, pressed up against the back of the shed. The man's feet were off the ground and his breathing was heavy. The striped sport coat and slacks he was wearing were scuffed and sullied from being tossed around a few times.

The one holding him, clean in the air like it was nothing, was

Marrok. He sneered into the man's desperate face. Next to him, a clean-cut leather jacket laid tossed to the ground by his firmly planted boots.

The stout man noticed her before Marrok did, and he reached toward her while his bulldog jowls pressed into Marrok's strong hands. "Please, miss. Get help."

Marrok socked him right in the jaw before letting him fall to the ground. He stood over him, chest heaving, before a smooth tilt of his head drew his attention to her.

Prairie couldn't move, let alone speak. But the moment she saw his eyes, reflecting back at her like a wild animal in the night, she hightailed it out of there. Her arms clutched her chest as she kept her focus to the ground and made sure her feet didn't stop moving.

She wasn't sure what to think. There was nothing crooked about Marrok before she saw him pinning that man. And despite him struggling to get away, Marrok didn't flinch, didn't even seem burdened by it. He was strong—much stronger than he looked.

Prairie made it to the concession stand and got back in line; her breath labored as she recovered from her escape. Flipping her hair, she looked back toward the playground, wondering what was happening now.

Maybe she should tell somebody. They'd try and stop him, not just try, but kick the tar out of him. A black man beating up a white man was not a picture most folks painted pretty. There must be a reason for it—one she wasn't too keen to find at the moment.

She got to the counter and grabbed some popcorn and drinks from the rack. She just needed to get back to the car and get lost in Connery's deep pooling eyes.

Her Mama was right. That curiosity of her's had walked her right into something she never wanted to be partial to. She was no Miss. Marple. She was a waitress.

She had to forget about what she saw. Because it wasn't her business. None of her business at all.

45

Chapter 8
The Apology

It was another slow morning at the Moonlight Diner. The sun was coming up over the trees, accompanied by the whisking of clouds that resembled the steam floating from a fresh pot of coffee.

Prairie kept her mouth shut about what she saw at the drive-in the night before, though she couldn't deny it kept her from having a restful sleep. Not that she was scared something would happen, no, instead she was more curious about why it happened. She couldn't imagine what Marrok was doing there pushing that man around like he owed him something. Maybe he did. It could be any number of reasons, and each of those reasons would keep anyone's mind racing for a triple crown victory like Citation.

And those eyes. Those unnatural glowing eyes.

Thinking about them sent shivers down her spine. They stuck out in her head like they meant something important: like maybe that man wasn't Marrok at all, just someone pretending to be him. It was silly to assume that based on what little she knew of him. His intentions were still so unclear. Everything about him was a dangerous game she was partially keen to play.

Prairie flipped through the pages of *Murder on the Orient Express.* Poirot's character was quite an unusual man, but even his witty remarks and curious debunking could not keep her distrac-

ted. With a huff, she lowered the book and looked out into the very empty diner. Placing it down so she wouldn't lose her spot, she pulled out her pad and a number 2 pencil from her apron. If words couldn't keep her mind still, then perhaps numbers would.

Prairie worked through the orders she took during the early morning hours and started tallying up her shift before her daddy came in. She wrote the amounts in the daily account book, which she pulled out from under the register, and left her initials in the margin. Only a handful of customers. She wouldn't be rolling in tips after a morning like this.

"Will you put mine in too, Prairie?" Bev slipped in beside her and leaned against the counter, flipping her curly brown hair out of her perfectly angled face. She slid Prairie her pad which Prairie took without question. With a single glance, Prairie's eyes grew double the size and she shot Bev a look.

"You get all these tips from a cup of coffee?"

Beverly smirked, tapping her lipstick against her cosmetics case before flipping it open. "What can I say? Those truckers appreciate a pretty girl leaning over the booth every once in a while."

Prairie continued to stare as Beverly finished painting her face. After a minute, Beverly noticed and closed the case. "What's that look for?"

"Does Georgie know you're doing all this?"

"Why would he care? As long as I bring in my share of the rent money, then who cares what I gotta do to get it."

Another minute of glaring and the two girls cracked with giddy laughter. Prairie wiped the joy from her eyes with a sigh as she started penciling in Beverly's night into the account book. "No wonder you can afford such nice things."

"You got it in you too, Prairie. You're just too polite." Bev leaned toward her. "Get a little frisky once in a while."

The door chimed open, and Beverly stood tall. "Mornin', Mr. Hemsworth."

Prairie looked up to see Bernard Hemsworth stroll through, wearing a plain brown suit and well-polished Oxfords. A copy of the morning paper was already under his arm, and a cigar hung from his mouth. Billy came shuffling in behind him. Single creased slacks and a plain button-up shirt with a checkered sport coat graced his finely tuned arms.

"Good morning to you too." Bernard looked at Prairie as she came off the counter. "Is your father in yet?"

"No, but he'll be in shortly."

"I'll wait." He glanced down the line of booths. "I'll be over there." He smacked the paper against Billy's chest, making him flinch. "Behave yourself, William." He didn't even wait for a response as he left Billy standing in the doorway while he took a comfortable seat at one of the booths.

Beverly's eyes flashed, looking from Billy to Prairie. "Guess I got one last customer. And a wealthy one at that." Taking back her pad, Bev grasped it and moved away from the counter. "I'll be good."

She sauntered over to Bernard's booth with a friendly smile. Shaking her head, Prairie went back to working over the book, trying to ignore Billy's slow approach toward the counter. He slipped into a seat and folded his hands in front of him.

"How have you been, Prairie?"

"Fine, no thanks to you." She pressed the lead into the page and glanced at Billy. "What's your uncle doing here, anyway?"

He shrugged. "Says he's trying to hook this place up with more state-of-the-art equipment."

"Like my daddy could afford that."

"That's what loans are for."

"A loan?" Prairie looked dead in Billy's eyes. "Your uncle is giving out loans now?"

Billy backed off the counter a little. "What's it to you?"

Prairie's mouth drew a line. She held her breath as Billy let out a sigh. "Come on, Prairie. You aren't really upset about my uncle now, are ya?"

"No. But I don't like him trying to peg money on my daddy that he could never pay back."

"Well, if he gets this place what it needs, maybe you'll make more of it."

Her hand curled around the pencil. "Don't you have anything better to say to me, Billy Hemsworth?"

Billy's tongue coated his top lip as he glanced over at his uncle's booth before coming back to watch his fingers twiddle. "I guess." He looked at her. "I apologize for trying to kiss you the other day."

Prairie's arms folded against her chest. "Is that all?"

"And . . . I wanted to ask you something." He adjusted his posture on the stool. "Your birthday is coming up real quick, and I wanted to know if . . . you'd let me take you out."

Prairie couldn't help but roll her eyes at him. He did not know when to let up. "What kind of apology is that? And no. You *cannot* take me out."

She dropped her arms and rushed from the counter toward the kitchen. Billy shot off the seat and followed her. "Come on, Prairie. Let me make it up to you and take you out. I won't try nothing." She made it to the swinging doors of the kitchen before he added, "Give me another chance."

Prairie stopped with her hands on the door. Her heart was beating for her to spit in his face and leave him dry. After what he tried to pull in the car, she shouldn't forgive him. There was no changing the Billy who hid under his uncle's wing.

But there were times the old Billy came out. The fun-loving, sweet Billy who managed to capture her attention, if only for a little while.

Elliot peaked out of the service window and looked from Prairie to Billy. He adjusted his specs with a smile. "Good morning to ya, Mr. Hemsworth."

"He's not Mr. Hemsworth." Prairie's hand slid from the door with a sigh. "He's just Billy."

She turned around, dropped her arms to her sides in defeat, and began tapping her pencil against her leg.

Billy leaned over the counter, "I'll make it right. Prairie I . . ." his voice grew real quiet.

". . . I miss you. I just . . . I need to do this for you. Please."

She searched his face; it was all sad like a puppy dog. He was reaching deep and trying to yank at the heartstrings that still pined for him. Prairie glanced behind him where Bernard had found a seat at one of the booths. He eyed them with a smug look on his face. He was making all sorts of judgements now, on Billy in particular.

She stepped closer to where Billy was at the counter, "He's been pushing you hard hasn't he?"

"Don't worry about what he's got me doing."

"I do worry," she sighed as she tapped her pencil against her leg. She should say no because it would end like everything else had ended lately. Beverly was right, she shouldn't be giving him hope, but maybe she hoped too. Hoped that she could reach in and pull out the Billy he used to be. It seemed clearer today than any other day that he was hoping she would. "Fine. You can take me out."

Billy's face lit up like a Christmas tree. "Great. And I won't mess it up. I promise, Prairie."

He grabbed her hand and squeezed it like he was ready to take her out right then.

"William!" Bernard ushered him over to the booth.

Billy raised a finger and nodded,. "I gotta go over." He turned back to Prairie. "I'll call you later?"

"Fine." She sighed, watching him hustle to the booth as she pocketed her pencil.

Prairie laid her back on the door and pushed it open. She dragged her feet to the sink before turning the knob to let the cool rush coat her hands. It didn't matter how many times Billy screwed up, she always gave in. She couldn't seem to harden the soft spot in her heart that he left with her since their first kiss on the bleachers after the big homecoming game junior year. And if it saved him from a night of having his uncle breathing down his neck, it was worth it.

"You ain't acting like a girl who's just been asked on a date by the richest boy in Oak Springs."

She leaned against the sink as Elliot cracked some eggs on to the grill, sizzling up a buttery scent. "Why should it matter if he's the richest boy or not?"

Elliot shrugged, shifting the potatoes from side to side with his metal spatula. "I guess it doesn't."

The morning continued as always. Commuters and visitors heading up to Albany stopped in to grab a quick bite. The last hour of work was always crazy like this before her parents showed up. Prairie was in the kitchen when they walked in. Bernard was already up to greet them, and he shook her daddy's hand and gave Ma a kiss on the cheek. It made her skin crawl seeing how well he seemed to get along with them, though she was sure it was just an act.

"I can't stand that man," she breathed, piling up the plates that just came clean from the sink. "He better not be filling daddy's head with nonsense."

"Come on, Prairie," Elliot placed some more orders in the window and rang the bell, "give Jerry some credit. He's not someone to just act without thinking."

"I suppose you're right."

Just then, Jerry came through the doors, waving the morning paper in his hand. "Have you seen the papers this morning?"

"What's that, Jerry?" Elliot's attention moved away from the grill.

"There's been another murder." Jerry flashed the first page and folded it at the crease. "See there?" Both Elliot and Prairie advanced toward the fine black and white print as Jerry continued on. "A man by the name of Lesley Darcy. A well-to-do from Albany. Found shot in a ditch somewhere off 43."

"Shot, huh?" Elliot's mouth turned in disappointment. "Don't match the others if he was shot." He went back to the grill without a second glance. Despite his lack of empathy for yet another man who met a sudden end, Prairie could not pull herself away from the paper.

Sitting right next to the headline was a picture of the man: stout and bald with bulldog jowls. Not a feature was out of place from when she saw him pressed up against the back of the shed at the drive-in—with Marrok's fingers wrapped around his throat.

Prairie backed away and pushed herself out the door into the diner. She made a line to the farthest corner, where a table was waiting to be cleared off. The top of the window was open, letting the fresh air in and the comforting smells of bacon and coffee out. Leaning against the wall, she took a deep breath, trying to quell the rush of her heartbeat.

Marrok killed him, she thought. *He killed that man.*

There wasn't a doubt in her mind—not a shred. There couldn't be any other explanation. The way his eyes shone like that; those weren't the ones looking at her from the driver's seat of his Thunderbird. Those were the eyes of someone looking for blood.

Should she go to the police?

"Neglecting your duties again for that *girl*?"

The familiar voice of Bernard pulled her to the window. He was walking with Billy to his well waxed Cadillac. Prairie stepped against the wall to keep out of sight. She pressed the side of her head to the wall to listen.

"She's not just any girl," Billy replied.

"She's in the way, William," she peaked over the edge to see them facing each other with Billy's back to the car door. "You have to stay the course."

"Get someone else to do your dirty work then. If it's so important—"

Benard's hand grabbed Billy's collar before he pushed him against the car. Prairie pulled herself away and held her hand to her mouth like they could hear her breathing.

"You're not a kid anymore," he said. "You want to get ahead? You have to toe the line and stop filling your head with girls like her. She's a liability, and when she sticks her pretty little nose in where it doesn't belong, the only one in the crosshairs will be you."

The weight of his words dropped Prairie's heart into her feet. She dared to look out the window again and saw Billy standing there with gritted teeth and clenched fists at his sides. He wanted to swing at him so bad, she could see the seething behind his eyes, but he wouldn't. Not ever. His uncle was all he had and pride in his family outweighed the treatment of those that were part of it.

Bernard eventually let him go. With that smug look about him, he adjusted his hat. "Now get in the car. We're late."

Prairie sank back against the wall. The air she kept in her lungs began to ache in her chest. She let it slowly drain from her lips, closing her eyes for a moment before she wiped her hands on her apron.

She didn't know what was worse, seeing Marrok roughing up that man who ended up dead, or seeing how much of a prisoner to his uncle Billy really was.

Chapter 9
The Dress

"What about this one?" Beverly pulled out a cute little dress from the rack of the Newcastle department store.

Prairie looked it over, admiring the floral pattern and overly accentuated bodice. "It doesn't scream at me."

"Well, it certainly screams something." She let it fall back into the sea of dresses. "You gotta pick something that will make Billy regret not asking you out sooner."

"He has." Prairie pressed a hand against her pinned back hair. "But I just couldn't say yes to him."

"Until now?" Bev shot her a raised brow. Prairie twisted her mouth at her friend's suggestive tone.

Thinking of Billy rolled back the conversation she overheard in the parking lot between him and his uncle. "Something's going on with him," she said, stopping just before the door. "I just . . . I want him to be okay."

"I know you care about him, otherwise you wouldn't keep him around," Beverly placed a hand on her arm. "You know what he's been through—more than me. He's worth saving to you, right?"

"I don't know if I'd call it saving."

They exited the department store and stepped onto the bust-

ling downtown sidewalk of Oak Springs. "If anyone can help him get his head on straight, it's you."

Prairie welcomed the vote of confidence Beverly was giving her, but even now, she wasn't so sure she could help him. But it wouldn't be from lack of trying.

Stores and eateries lined both sides of the street. Cars parked on every corner and meters ran day and night. This was the happening place to be for most of the residents of Oak Springs, and the ideal place to find a dress perfect for her upcoming birthday date.

They walked up to a lamppost where a strapping young man in his teddy boy getup stood. He had combed up hair and a distinguished chin that made him look more like a movie star than a salesman. He turned as they approached, grinning ear to ear. Bev fell from Prairie's arm and threw herself at him. She kissed him all swoony like. "We didn't keep you waiting too long, did we?"

"Not at all." Georgie looked up at Prairie. "Find anything yet?"

She shook her head, uncrossing her arms before she reached up to pull her cat eye sunglasses from her head back down to her eyes. "Not yet."

Bev turned to her and leaned against Georgie with a grin. "Why don't we try Clark's? They got a lot of nice ones in the shop window."

"Can we stop at that pastry shop first?" Georgie asked. "My stomach's growling just thinking about it."

Prairie laughed. "I don't wanna keep you waiting for me. I'll meet you if you wanna head down there."

"Prairie, I said I would help you find something." Bev moved away from Georgie. "You can't pawn me off just yet."

"I'm not pawning you off. I just want to look by myself for a bit."

Beverly sighed and flipped her long hair over her right shoulder. Georgie took her hand. "You're not exactly modest, Bev."

Her hand playfully batted his chest. "Hush, you." She came

back to Prairie. "All right, but don't buy anything till I take a look at it."

"Fine, I'll drag you over once I find something I like."

"Want me to get you anything from the pastry shop, Prairie?" Georgie asked.

"If they got any of those strawberry rhubarb pies, the little ones?"

"Sweet and sharp. It's how you like most things, huh, Prairie?" Beverly said as she and Georgie made for the curb.

Prairie waved them off and headed left at the corner. "I'll meet you over there."

Her yellow polka dotted dirndl whisked behind her as she walked down the street. She rounded the corner along the side of the Newcastle department store. A pair of drinking fountains stood to her right, each labeled in bold letters: *White Only* and *Colored Only*. She stopped in front of them, staring at the letters as if they had a voice all their own. Nothing would happen to her if she drank from the colored fountain, except maybe a slap on the wrist and a few choice remarks. If a colored man or woman, or god forbid a child, drank from the white only fountain, however . . .

A man in a derby cap stepped in beside her, "Excuse me, miss."

"Oh, sorry." She moved out of the way so he could quench his thirst. He leaned over the white only fountain. Prairie adjusted her purse around her wrist and continued on, shaking the thoughts right out of her head. It wasn't like she'd never seen a fountain like that before, but ever since Marrok, it had become more than just a fountain. Or a sign. Or whatever it was that drew her attention to the small little details of her everyday life. Like everything that kept her world together wasn't really doing a good job at all.

As she passed a tiny eatery with outdoor seating, a man who was reading the paper stood up. "Miss. O'Shea."

Prairie turned to find the tan-coated detective folding up his paper before tucking it under his arm. A cigarette hung in his mouth as he stepped onto the sidewalk.

"Detective Greenway." She held her breath, tilting her head forward as he approached. "To what do I owe the pleasure?"

His ruffed face stretched into a grin as he pulled the smoke from his lips. "I take it you've heard about . . . recent events."

She watched him cooly, trying to keep herself from blurting out anything she would regret. "That murder, I suppose you mean? And what's that got to do with me?"

"Nothing at all." He gestured for her to continue on to wherever it was she was heading. Prairie eyed him as she walked away, but Greenway stepped in beside her.

"But it may have something to do with your drifter." He turned to her. "Has he been back to your diner?"

Prairie shook her head, casting her gaze forward with her jaw locked. "No, sir. He hasn't been there since." Everything inside of her screamed to tell him what she saw and about how she was sure he killed that man at the drive-in and maybe all the others along that stretch of road.

"Any eyes on him at all? Even outside your diner?"

Prairie stopped. She was getting the feeling that he knew more than he was letting on. Had he been following her? Did he know that Marrok gave her a ride to work that day? Maybe it was fruitless to keep things to herself. He was the one who could dig up more than her. She was just some girl who couldn't keep her curiosity from getting the better of her.

Despite how things seemed to connect, that feeling lingered: that Marrok wasn't the one they were looking for. Clenching her teeth, she turned to him, relieved that she was still wearing her sunglasses. "What exactly do you want from me, Detective?"

Greenway placed the smoke back in his mouth. "Just hoping

you're the kind of person who'd speak up if the man wanted for these murders showed his face again."

"What makes you think he's done it at all?"

"More than you'd care to know, Miss. O'Shea."

She looked down at the sidewalk, folding her arms and leaning to one side.

Those startling eyes that seemed to mirror the night sky as Marrok had his hand wrapped around that man's neck came creeping up from her memories. They were unnatural, like something you'd see traipsing through the woods on a moonless night. When he gave her a ride to the diner, they were anything but. Guarded and sad, but not a killer. There was no way to know for sure. So, until she knew, she'd keep her trap shut. Even if he was who Greenway wanted. She wouldn't be the one to tell.

"I got your card, Mr. Greenway." She turned to him again. "Unless you plan on taking me in, I'd like to continue my day without you tailing me about stuff I don't know a lick about."

A low chuckle shook his chest. "Fair enough, Miss. O'Shea." He tipped his hat to her.

"You have a nice day now."

He turned and left. Prairie watched him until he disappeared around the corner from where she came. He was waiting for her, or so it seemed. Prairie tried to pry the thought from her mind as she continued on toward Clark's. None of this had anything to do with her. She had to keep telling herself that.

Just the thought of Marrok sent her stomach a flutter. The butterflies battered the inside of her like wind cutting through a pile of leaves.

When she finally reached Clark's, she stopped in front of the shop window. A few mannequins stood all dolled up in their display. One of them wore a plain blue dress with a slim white belt.

The skirt flared just enough. Two strings tied at the top, resting on the shoulders, and the neck wasn't too low.

She took a step to the window, imagining herself wearing it with white daisies in her hair to match the belt. Though she was shopping for a dress for her date with Billy, she couldn't help but think about what Marrok would say if he saw her in it.

"You're it." She said to herself.

Billy would gush all over her in this dress, not that he wouldn't if she were just wearing her waitress uniform.

Marrok wouldn't be as forward as Billy, who was just looking for a chance to compliment her. Would he outright say if she looked nice? Or just think it? He was guarded, but maybe that was to protect himself. From what, she could only guess. Surely, he would say something.

A whistle of air escaped her as she shook her head. *You think too much.*

A high-pitched laugh caught her attention. Prairie looked down the road and saw a car parked at the corner. A colored girl in a pink blouse and high waisted pedal pushers leaned in the window. She was chatting up someone whose face was half covered in the shadow.

Prairie narrowed her eyes as they shifted into the sun. She blinked twice, not sure who she was seeing, but something about the way his hair was brushed and his wide-mouthed smile seemed awfully familiar. It wasn't long before the window rolled up and the car drove away. The girl straightened, glancing in her direction before walking across the street and out of sight.

A sudden thought tumbled to mind. *Billy talking to a colored girl?*

No, it must have been someone else. The car didn't look anything like Billy's. There were plenty of fellas who adopted his Cheshire grin, if only to make themselves appear charming.

Prairie turned and stepped into Clark's, distracting herself with the thought of trying on the perfect dress.

Chapter 10
The Songbird

Jerry grabbed his wallet from the desk and slipped it in his jacket pocket. Prairie waited patiently by the door, observing his furrowed brow and the loose strands of his hair swaying into his eyes.

"Daddy?" She spoke calmly as Jerry's gaze shot up to meet her.

"Prairie." He combed his hair back with his fingers and sighed. "What can I help you with?"

She took a step into the office. There was a lot on her mind since seeing that man's face in the papers. As much as that kept her awake in her bed each night, there was something else.

"Billy told me something the other day." Her hands fell into her apron. "About Mr. Hemsworth and your dealings."

Jerry's lips folded as he weighed his words. Prairie didn't want to believe her daddy would do something as foolish as borrowing money from that man. Their relationship with the Hemsworth's was always pleasant when Billy's folks were alive, but that had changed, just like Billy had.

"You taking money from him?"

Jerry smoothed his lapel. "It's nothing you need to worry about."

"Daddy." Prairie closed the gap between them. "You can't take money from him. He's crooked."

"Crooked?" Jerry expelled a breath-filled smile. "He's a Hemsworth. We're practically family."

"When Billy's mama and daddy were alive, I'd agree with you, but . . ." She stopped herself before letting her opinion overtake her. She was free to speak her mind with her daddy, but this seemed different than any other situation. The last thing she wanted was for her folks to owe a cent to that man. Even when she was a child, she was always cautious of Bernard Hemsworth.

"Where did this come from, Prairie?" Jerry asked.

"I just . . ." she clenched her teeth. "I just don't like him is all. And the thought of you owing him anything makes my skin crawl."

"The diner's barely hanging on, Prairie. I don't know how much longer we can manage it with how things are going." Jerry placed a gentle hand on her shoulder and gave her a weak smile. "But I promise, I haven't agreed to anything yet. It's a big decision, and I want to make sure it's the right one for this place and our family."

Prairie saw the truth in his matching green eyes. She trusted him more than anyone, and if he said he didn't take money from Bernard Hemsworth, she had to believe him. "Okay, Daddy."

Jerry wiped a finger over her freckled cheek. "That's my girl." He turned back and relinquished his coat from the back of his chair. "So, what's this I hear about Billy taking you out on your birthday?"

Prairie leaned back on her heels. "It's nothing special."

"What do you mean nothing special?" He threw his coat over his shoulder. "Sure sounds special to me." He nudged her to the door to follow.

Prairie fell in beside him as they slowly walked into the kitchen. "I don't know. He's not been the same since his folks died."

"But you like him?"

"I do, but . . ." She leaned into Jerry's arm.

"A lot is expected of him now. Taking the reins of a family business isn't without its challenges, and Bernard isn't the most . . . understanding when it comes to spying weakness."

They pushed through the kitchen. "It's a good thing he has you."

"You think?" Prairie walked onto the diner floor, with her daddy not far behind. "I don't feel that way half the time."

"Listen, sugar pie." Jerry faced her, leaning against the front door to the parking lot. "Billy is going through a lot. I know it's been a year, but a loss like that changes you. I can't say it hasn't changed me. Desmond was . . . a good friend."

She placed a comforting hand on his arm. "I know you miss him."

"I do. Every day." Jerry peered out the window into the waning light behind the trees. "But having someone to lean on from time to time, to help you forget about all the pain that you're still holding onto. . ." He turned to her, "Sometimes that's all a person needs to want to keep moving forward."

Prairie never thought about Billy needing her for anything but trying to get a kiss in, but what her daddy said made all the sense in the world. "I suppose you're right."

"Good." He put an arm around her and squeezed her tight. "Now that doesn't mean he doesn't need to treat you right."

"I can handle him, Daddy."

"I know you can." He placed a kiss on the top of her head before letting his arm slip from her back. "I'll see you in the morning."

"Love you."

"Love you too, sugar pie."

Jerry let himself out through the door. As he walked to his car, Prairie let her mind wander to the other secrets she'd kept from him. She should have told him about the detective confronting her on the street, or that she saw the man in the papers in the hands of the drifter he had warned her to be cautious of, or even that she thought she saw Billy talking to an unlikely sort of girl.

There was no reason to worry him. He had enough on his plate with the diner performing so poorly. When it was all over, she'd tell him everything, including how silly she was for thinking it was all tied together somehow.

The diner was quiet. Beverly was under the weather and called out of work, so only Elliot was with her this morning. A few cops had already come and gone, grabbing a bite and a coffee before continuing their patrols up and down the highway. Prairie did her customary wiping of the tables, even though they hadn't been sat in for some time.

Turning the corner toward the final group of booths, her gaze landed on the jukebox. Her fingers ran over the domed glass, looking over the songs that lived inside. She had to do something to take her mind off everything and singing was the best way she knew how.

Ella Fitzgerald's name loosened the strain of her eyes. Pressing down on her selection, she watched the record rise and fall onto the turntable. The needle touched down ever so gently and scratched out the fuzz before letting the queen of jazz spin to life.

Prairie loved the soul she heard in Ella's voice. She always sang from the heart, which was something she admired. Prairie closed her eyes, letting the song unfold, breaking through her thoughts as the words leaked from her lips.

It had been a while since she caught herself singing. Her folks loved her voice, but they were the only ones she would sing for. Singing in front of people, despite her outward personality, left her so rattled she forgot how to stand. It was one of the few things she was afraid to admit.

"You showin' off now, miss?"

Prairie's eyes shot open, her shoes squeaking as she turned. Marrok sat in a booth to her left, smoke billowing from the butt of a cigarette and wafting across his deep brown skin. Her hand landed on her chest as she leaned into the jukebox.

"What'd I tell you 'bout calling me miss?"

"My mistake." He leaned forward on the table against his crossed arms. Prairie was sure she was alone. She checked all the booths before pitching on a song. There wasn't a moment that the mystery surrounding this man didn't grow.

"Something wrong?" He asked as she came away from the glass.

"No." She breathed. "You just startled me, that's all." She couldn't wrap her head around how he came in without her noticing. Or Elliot. He would have roared his head off the second Marrok walked in. "How did you get in here?"

He gestured toward the emergency exit door to the left of the jukebox, "You best get that door fixed."

Prairie swallowed, feeling like a fool for not noticing him sitting there while she waltzed on by, lost in her own head. "Why are you here?"

He pulled out a card of matches, "Why do you think I'm here?"

She wiped her hands on the rag hanging from her apron. The drive-in. The dead man in the paper.

"It wasn't any of my business. I didn't see anything." She was so uneasy she wasn't sure she could stand being around him, though part of her wanted nothing more.

"I got work to do," she said as she hurried back toward the front of the diner, but when she came to pass by his table, his hand came up and grasped her arm. Not in a way that would suggest malicious intent, but only to garner her attention and stop her in her tracks.

"You're scared of me."

Prairie wasn't expecting the soft feel of his hand on her skin raising the hairs on the back of her neck, "I'm not scared."

"You are." Marrok's gaze shifted upward to meet her eyes. "I can smell it on ya."

They waited, neither batting an eye nor shifting a flick. Prairie remained posed as she listened to her pulse beating like mad against her temples.

Marrok looked to the right, toward the other end of the diner. She was hoping to see that glint again, but it wasn't there. Had she imagined it? It hadn't crossed her mind until then, that maybe it was all in her head. Was her mind making Marrok into something grander than just a man?

"You gonna holler up there?" He asked, keeping his voice steady.

She shook her head, pressing her lips together as she tried to calm the surge of nerves from her lungs. He looked at the bench across from him. Prairie slowly moved into the booth and his hand slid down her arm as she sat across from him.

She watched him reach into his jacket for a pack. He yanked a stick out with his teeth before lighting it up with a single strike against the window frame. He brought it to his mouth and the tip glowed as he inhaled the nicotine into his lungs before letting it steadily escape from his nostrils.

"That man ended up dead." His voice was calm. "It was all over them papers."

Prairie's words caught in her throat. She watched him, his eyes intently on her. Aside from knowing if she squealed, she didn't understand why he was here. What did it matter what she thought about the whole thing? She was a nobody. Just a girl who was too curious for her own good about a colored man she couldn't keep out of her head.

She took a deep breath, relaxing her arms. "I'm not afraid of you, really," Prairie watched him for a minute, wondering if her prying was another reason for him to find her. "What were you doing . . . that night?"

His throat cleared as he lowered his smoke. "I was just taking out the trash." He sniffed. "I was lookin' for information, and he gave me lip. So, I roughed him up a bit."

"So, roughing people up? That's your business?"

"Sometimes."

She folded her hands together on the table. "Are you in a gang or something?"

Marrok blew another plume of smoke toward the window. "Why do you need to know?"

Prairie shook her head, her voice rising to her near bafflement. "You came here wanting to know something, didn't you? What I'm doing or thinking about all the questions hanging around you?"

He tapped his stick with his thumb, dropping ash into the tray on the table. "You keep showin' up is why."

"I don't mean to. It just . . . happens," she bit the inside of her lip, "The cops already got their finger pointed at you."

He scoffed, "I ain't worried about no badge."

"You should be," she pressed her palms into the table, "from that man ending up dead and your bloody arm. All those murdered on 43 were pulled from the car windows."

His hands dropped with a thud, startling Prairie out of her skin, "If you think I'd done it, then why not turn me in?"

"Because," she dropped her chin, realizing her volume was turning up something fierce. "I don't know," she let all the tension out with a sigh. "I just have a feeling, is all."

"A feelin'," that southern drawl of his sank him back into the blue upholstery of the seat, "not many white girls would stand on the side of a black man with just a feelin' to go by."

"Well, I'm not many white girls, I guess." Her forest green eyes met his soft brown, "I'd stand up for anyone who can't stand up for themselves. It's how it should be. It's what's right."

A huff drew up a grin. Marrok leaned his head to one-side, keeping his eyes on her. Him looking at her made her heart skip something terrible. She could feel it bash against her ribs like a screen door in a thunderstorm. Prairie brushed invisible hair behind her ears, forcing herself to look away. She could feel his eyes on her. How he was looking, not judging, but almost admiringly so. She didn't know why she was so embarrassed, him looking at her like that.

Beverly's words suddenly sprang to mind.

He was handsome . . . like if James Dean was colored. Cool, tough and drenched from the rain.

"You got the voice of a songbird."

His compliment brought her back to the conversation. She could feel the heat lighting up the freckles dotting her face as she rested her hands on the table in front of her. "Thank you for saying so."

"You ever think of singing on stage?" Marrok drew another hit off his cigarette. "You'd be a natural."

She shook her head. "No. I . . . can't do that. I get too nervous."

"You ever try?"

She pressed her lips together. "Can't say I have."

"Then how do you know?"

"I don't know." She shrugged. "Just the thought gets me all jittery."

He smiled. "Then don't think about it. Just go up there and do it."

"It ain't that easy." Prairie eyed him carefully. "Maybe for you southern boys. I don't have a shred of confidence in my body."

Marrok leaned off the seat. "You stand up for other people, but not for yourself?"

Her eyes shifted from the table to the window. He was prying just like she had pried him. They each had the other's attention now. It both rattled her bones and sent her heart skipping like a pebble across a pond. When she could find the courage to look at him again, the corner of his lip twitched upward.

Prairie felt the need to compliment him, but she kept it tightly inside, not wanting to come off all flirty like. It was hard not to indulge herself. It was like those honey-brown eyes pulled that side out of her. "That's just the kind of girl I am, I suppose."

That twitch turned into a smile that could knock out any girl's heart. "I know exactly what kind of girl you are." He leaned against the table, snuffing his cigarette into the ashtray.

Every word that ran from his tongue shortened her breath and kept the butterflies fluttering. Her heart was beating so hard she thought it'd jump out of her chest. Prairie fussed with her hair, face aglow.

"How do you know?"

His hands slid back from the table. "Just a feelin'."

He was loosening up, indulging her words with his own smooth kind of talking that left her wanting more. There wasn't anything she didn't want to know about this man. He had her attention from the start, and she didn't have the strength to look away. How he saw her just added to the mystery of who he was or what he was doing in this quiet little corner of upstate New York.

There was still so little she understood. So many questions fluttered around him like fall leaves on a windy morning. She couldn't help but think of something she read in one of her books; *is this what Christie meant about stumbling upon a coincidence?*

"Actually," she let her words break through her thoughts. "I wanted to go to school. To become a nurse."

"Why didn't you?"

Her gaze fell over the diner. "Diner's not doing too good. Mama and Daddy need the help and can't afford to send me. So, I'm working here till I can save up."

"How long will that take ya?"

Prairie settled back on his still and concentrated form. "Long."

Marrok huffed. "Like a bird in a cage wantin' to fly. How hard you gotta flap those wings of yours until they break them bars?"

"Why do you care if I get out or not? It doesn't affect you."

He pointed at her. "You deserve to live the life you want. Everybody does. Whether you're white like you," His finger turned to hover just below his eyes. "Or black like me."

Prairie pressed her palm across her mouth and turned to look at her reflection in the window. Every minute that ticked by on the clock of the diner stirred her up so much, she couldn't see straight. Nothing he said was for nothing. Not to her.

Closing her eyes, she dragged her palm down her chin before opening to catch his. "And what about you? You always saw yourself doing what you do?"

"Can't say I have." He tucked his hands under his opposite elbows, hunkering down as if the weather got cold all of a sudden. "But my options are . . . limited. So, I do what I can. Find something good from the hand God dealt me."

"You got a good heart." The words slipped from her mouth before she could think to say them.

Marrok let go a breath-filled chuckle, looking down at the table before catching her eye. "That right?"

"I . . . I don't know, I just . . ." her hands came over her eyes, pressing at the corners, "I'm sorry. I don't know when to keep my mouth from flapping off."

"That's all right by me."

The bell from the front rang through the diner. Prairie straightened her posture, glancing behind before coming back to the table. "I gotta get back to work." She stood with a sigh. "Can I get you anything?"

"Much obliged." He leaned back to meet her, "But I think I got everything I need." He reached in his jeans pocket and pulled out some change then set it on the table.

"You don't have to pay for anything."

"For your time," he grinned, "it's worth somethin'."

Prairie came over and took it under her palm, barely gracing the tips of his fingers. It sent fireworks up her arm before shooting down her spine. Collecting it in her fist, she shoved it inside her apron. She took a shaky breath, jittering the chill that seemed to wake up her bones.

"You drive safe now."

"Have a good night." He nodded. "Miss. Prairie."

Chapter 11
The Date

Antione's was the fanciest restaurant in downtown Oak Springs and the most expensive. The old red brick structure was blanketed with dark green vines along the bottom, leading up to the thick heavy doors with brass cast window dressings. Even from outside, the smell of the rich red sauce and pastries this place was famous for wafted down the street. Prairie wasn't surprised when Billy rolled into the parking lot. He stepped out of the driver's side, handed the valet his keys, and walked over to her side to open the door for her.

He was wearing a clean-cut button-down shirt, open at the top, with a tweed jacket, and brown slacks. His light brown hair was duck tailed, with a few strands too short to pull back dangling on his forehead. As he opened the door, she got a quick shot of his pungent cologne mixed with the cool air of the summer night.

He held out his hand, which she took graciously, keeping the lavish blue of her dress up to avoid getting stuck as she passed through the door. She did her hair in the usual way, light mahogany curls and her favorite flowers tucked in the folds of her thick fringe.

Billy offered her his arm with a smirk, "I didn't think you could look prettier than you already do."

Prairie scoffed, slipping her arm in the crux of his elbow. "You don't need to flatter me, Billy." They walked around the car to the front of the restaurant. "And why take me here? It's too much."

"Come on. Don't you think you need to be spoiled every once in a while? It's not every day you turn 20 years old, is it?"

They walked up to the host, who smiled in his finely pressed tux as he ushered them to a private table overlooking the rose-strewn courtyard. It was too chilly to sit outside, but the night was still awfully pretty to look at from the window. It was dim, with only flickering oil lamps and candles as the source of light. A piano sat a few tables up, its keys gently stroked by another sharply dressed man to add to the atmosphere. Cigarettes smoked from ashtrays as patrons sipped on red wine and dined on freshly made pasta.

"Thank you." Prairie smiled as the host pushed in her seat. Billy sat across from her, adjusting his jacket as he settled into the red cushioned chair.

"Anything to drink this evening?" The host asked as he placed the menu on the table.

"It's a special night, so how 'bout we start with a bottle of chardonnay." Billy looked at Prairie as the host nodded.

"Certainly, Mr. Hemsworth. Your waiter will be over in just a moment." He left to fetch the wine.

Prairie took in the mood of the restaurant. She had only eaten here once before, a long time ago with her parents. Nothing had changed since then, except perhaps the prices. As she reached for the menu, Billy snatched it up.

"Don't you know a gentleman always orders for his date?"

"This ain't a date, Billy." She reached for it again, but Billy brought it to his chest.

"Even so, I'm taking *you* out. Not the other way 'round." He opened the menu to observe the offerings of the night.

Prairie leaned her elbow on the table and fell into her hand. "When are you gonna stop this, Billy?"

"I'll stop when you tell me to stop."

Her head came off her hand. "I *have* told you to stop. You don't wanna listen."

He peered at her from the menu. "Would you have said yes to coming out with me if you really didn't want to?"

She twisted her ruby-shaded lips and glanced out the window. Liking Billy felt like an instinct. He was like a brother and a friend to her. Her best friend if she was being honest with herself. It didn't become anything more until high school, and there were times she missed how playful and sweet they had been with each other during those times . . . before his parent's accident.

"What are you thinking about?" Billy asked as Prairie's gaze strayed back to him.

She leaned her chin in her palm. "Just . . . us. I suppose." Her hand fell to the table. "How we were."

Billy seemed to perk up at the prospect of strolling down memory lane. "I still remember the day I first asked you to be my girl."

Prairie smirked, her eyes straying to the light reflecting off her glass. "You didn't exactly ask me, Billy."

"I didn't have to now, did I?" He leaned his elbow on the table. "All I had to do was give you my letterman, and you practically jumped in my arms."

Prairie found herself blushing at the thought of how smitten she was with him back then. Billy was the first boy she ever liked in that way, and the only boy she thought she wanted.

"You were different then." He continued. "A little looser. Carefree maybe."

"We were both different." Prairie sighed. "We aren't like that anymore."

"But we could be."

Prairie pressed her mouth into a line, her hands coming together at the edge of the table. Nobody could turn back time. Even if they could, it didn't matter. She didn't feel that way anymore, not all the time. But sometimes . . . it came back. Like the kiss of a tide on your bare feet.

Through her contemplation, Billy set the menu down. "I got you something." He reached into the inside pocket of his jacket and pulled out a velvet bag with a string. "It's not much but, I thought you'd like it." He slid it in her direction. "Happy birthday."

Prairie looked at the bag, and her stomach tightened. "Billy, you didn't have to get me anything."

"But I did. And I'm not taking it back." He sat up from his chair and came beside her, taking the bag in his hand. "Open your hand."

Prairie carefully laid her hand out on the table. Billy pulled the string loose, emptying the contents into her palm. It was a necklace. The silver chain caught the flickering candlelight from the table. A beautiful green stone pendant hung at the center. Similar smaller stones lined two by two beside it, reflecting in the waning light.

"Emerald," She looked at Billy as he spoke. "To match your eyes."

Prairie brought the necklace closer to her, examining the newness of it, finding it hard to breathe. "Billy, this must have cost you a fortune."

"Nothing I can't afford." He placed his fingers in her hand. "May I?"

He didn't wait for her to answer as he picked up the necklace and came behind her. Prairie held up her hair for him to place it across her neckline. The pendant sat perfectly against the paleness of her skin. Her fingers ran over the stones as he stepped back to admire her.

"It looks perfect on you."

She laid her hands in her lap, trying to keep her heart from sputtering too fast. It was times like this she saw the old Billy in him. Not the pushy puppet his uncle had strung him up to be. It was this Billy, the one standing in front of her, that she let herself fall in love with years ago. "You're too good to me." She smiled.

Billy bent down and took her hand, kissing it gently. "And you're too good for me, but I'll take that smile any day over you swinging at me."

"I wouldn't swing at you if you didn't deserve it."

"I know. You keep me from slipping, Prairie." He let go of her hand. "You always have."

The host came over with the wine. Billy didn't take his eyes off her as he sat back in his seat. Even with the glasses being poured and resting in front of them, Prairie couldn't shake herself free from the moment. Because at this moment, she thought Billy could steal her heart.

Something she never thought would happen again.

Chapter 12
The Dive

Dinner was a dream, peppered with the usual cheeky banter, but it didn't bother Prairie this time. Not a lick. Billy whipped out that youthful charm he kept in his back pocket, and it was rubbing off on her real quick.

"You want to order anything else?" Billy asked after they finished a perfect dessert of tiramisu.

"I couldn't eat another bit," Prairie dabbed her mouth with the cloth napkin. "It was delicious."

"Only the best for you."

The piano readied itself for the next tune. It only took the first few notes to strike for Prairie's eyes to light up. She looked from where the piano sat, tucked to the right of the restaurant, and Billy.

"Is this," she held up her hand, pointing gingerly as the music played, "it is. It's Earth Angel, isn't it?"

Billy pushed out his chair, coming over to stand next to her with a hand out. "Special request," he smiled, "if you'd like to dance?"

She didn't waste a blink, taking his hand and letting him lead her to the small dance space for anyone looking to stretch their legs to a tune. Billy took her hand into his as she placed the other on his shoulder. His free hand came to her waist.

"Junior prom," he said, "remember?"

"I remember," matching his smile with a grin of her own. "You kissed me when we were dancing to this song."

"You sure," his eyes squinted with mild surprise, playing up the jib, "that wasn't someone else?"

Prairie squeezed his arm, leaning closer to him, "If it was, you would have decked them right then and there."

They each shared in the jest, smiling with their eyes, and chuckling together. This was the Billy she remembered. The one she was fighting to see. It had been so long since he let this side of him shine, and she couldn't get enough of it. She wanted to hold on to it forever and protect him from anyone who sought to bury it in the cold, hard ground.

When the song ended, Prairie dragged her hand down his arm to catch his hand escaping her waist. She squeezed it, keeping it tight in her palm, "I missed this," she smiled, fixing his hair like she used to do. "I missed you."

He wiped his thumb across her cheek and let it linger at the corner of her mouth, "It could be like this again. Just like this."

She wanted to believe him, but this was only a glimpse, the first she'd seen in over a year. Now, it seemed more possible than ever. But still *only* possible. There was a lot to make up for, and Prairie would be fooling herself if she thought it could happen so quickly. She had to be patient, and so did he.

"I hope so. One day."

Billy drew his hand from her face, taking a step back. "Ready to split?"

Prairie was relieved he didn't try anything else. That would have been the wrong move. But this Billy wasn't looking to do anything wrong by her. Maybe he was finally realizing that now.

After he took care of the check, he offered her his coat as they stepped out into the night. "I should have brought a cardigan." She said as Billy settled his sport coat across her shoulders.

"You sure you weren't hoping I'd do this?" She pushed at him playfully as he slipped his arm across her shoulders. They walked down the path toward the parking lot. The valet stood in his maroon uniform, ready to fetch their car at a moment's notice.

"Could we walk a bit?" Prairie asked.

"Sure." Billy looked at the valet. "Is it okay if we leave the car here?"

The man smiled and nodded graciously. "Of course. As long as you're back before closing time."

"We will be." Billy grabbed a coin from his back pocket and flipped it toward him. The valet caught it, brought it to his chest, and tipped his hat. "Thank you much, Mr. Hemsworth."

They headed down the street toward the line of brick-and-mortar storefronts and restaurants. Downtown Oak Springs was a bustling place this time of night on a weekend. Most of the restaurants were jam packed with smoke so thick you'd think you were catching a steam-powered train. It was much quieter now, being a Thursday, the perfect night to enjoy the company without distractions.

Streetlamps hummed as they passed underneath them. Prairie leaned into Billy's shoulder a bit, enjoying the silence. She couldn't get over how much she was dreading this. She had tried to convince herself that it was a mistake, but he kept his promise. He didn't try anything. A true gentleman.

They approached the Newcastle Department Store display window. Dim lights silhouetted the mannequins as they stood poised in place. The same outfits she saw them in a few days before still clung to their plastic bodies. Prairie shifted against Billy, the sight of the store bringing up a question she was keen to get an answer on.

"I thought I saw you the other day." She said as they continued on their walk.

"Maybe you did. What was I doing?" Billy's voice was calm and soft, not in the least bit concerned with her question.

Prairie pulled away from him a tad so she could get a good look at him. "You were talking to someone. Real friendly like."

Billy's arm tightened around her. "As friendly as this?"

"Not quite." He squeezed a giggle from her. Prairie took a quick breath to regain her composure. "I thought it odd, you talking to a colored girl—"

Billy's arm dropped suddenly from across her shoulders, his mouth twisting as he sniffed in the cool air through his nostrils. "I ain't ever flirted with any jezebel. Not ever. You think I would do that? Mingle with those kinds of girls?"

Prairie's grip on his jacket tightened. "Calm down, Billy. I only thought—"

"Well, you thought wrong." Billy's eyes shifted as he turned to grab her. "You best get your eyes checked if you'd ever think I'd breathe in the same direction as one of them. Now take it back."

"Take it back?" Prairie hardened her jaw, pressing her brow upon her eyes. "What's gotten into you? Why are you acting like this?"

He narrowed his stare. "Take it back, Prairie."

With a quick shove, she backed away from him. "I most certainly will *not* take it back. It *was* you. Otherwise, why'd you be acting like this?"

"You know what mingling with dirt will do to a man's reputation? A man like me? Unlike you, I give a damn. You . . . waltzing into that greaser's car like he wasn't negro scum."

Prairie pulled his jacket off her shoulders with a huff. "How dare you judge anybody by something so petty." She swiped at his hand, smacking it away. "And you best get that finger out of my face."

Billy went rigid, the deep rise and fall of his chest the only thing keeping him from yelling. Prairie felt her eyes water, exacerbating her heart.

"You said I keep you from slipping? Well, you best knock off whatever it is you're up to if you want me to see you as anything other than the scum you speak of." She turned on her heels, clashing them on the ground as she tried to walk away as quickly as possible. This man, he wasn't Billy anymore.

She didn't get very far before Billy grabbed her wrist, twisting her around to face him. She let his jacket fall from her arm, tightening her muscles so he couldn't wretch it more. "Where you going?"

"Away from you. I don't need your permission to leave. Now, let go of me."

"Not until you take it back."

Prairie tightened her lips to hold back the dam behind her eyes. "Let go of me."

Billy pulled her toward him. "Why you gotta push my buttons? Just take it back!"

"Let. Me. Go. Now." She spoke through gritted teeth.

Something came out from the shadows of the alley, grabbing Billy by the shoulder with smooth caution. "You best listen to the lady."

Prairie's eyes flashed as she looked at the man in his teddy boy attire. Dark pants and jacket complemented his pale button-down. A tie hung undone around his neck and a fedora hid his dark, smoking face. When Billy let her go, wheeling around like a roller skate, Prairie's heart stopped as the fedora came up to reveal Marrok's deep brown eyes.

"How dare you put your hands on me!" Billy jerked away from him, planted his feet on the ground, and bared his teeth. "Get outta here or I'll drop you."

Marrok took a slow step back, his Camel dropping to the ground before snuffing it out between his Oxfords. "I'd like to see you try, slick."

Billy rolled up his sleeves. "You'll be diggin' your own grave if you mess with me."

"Am I now?" Marrok shifted in his stance, rolling his tongue against the inside of his lower lip.

Billy up and swung a fist square toward his jaw, but Marrok caught it in his hand and held it steady with unwavering eyes. Billy's face pressed as he gritted his teeth to try to force it forward, but no matter how much pressure he put behind his fist, it didn't budge. Marrok got real close to his straining face, never blinking, trained and focused. It was then she saw it again, that flash of light coating the brown of his eyes. It jumped Prairie's heart into her throat, making it impossible to breathe.

Her mind flashed back to the drive-in. Marrok's hand around that pudgy man's throat, squeezing the life out of him, only for him to end up dead. She still didn't know if Marrok was the one who did it. He said he didn't, and she believed him. But in this moment, seeing that same predatory look, she couldn't help but think he was more than capable of it.

Holding her breath tight in her lungs, she forced her feet to move beside Billy. "Stop this. *Now!*"

Prairie yanked on him. Marrok let go as Billy recoiled his hand to his chest, taking a few steps back. "You best watch your back, spook. I ain't afraid of you." He glanced at Prairie. "Come on."

"I'm not going anywhere with you." She took in a short breath, letting the first tear fall. "What's going on with you, Billy? You're like two different people. I . . . I don't recognize you half the time. Ever since your parents—"

Billy sneered. "You don't know anything about it, so stop pretending you do."

"I would if you talked to me. We could tell each other anything and now . . . and now . . . you are hiding things from me. I wanna help you."

"You only care about yourself. Stop acting like you give a lick about me." He bent down to pick up his jacket. "You're a piece of work, Prairie. A real thick piece of work."

His hand shot out and grabbed the necklace he gifted her, ripping it off. The clasp clinked on the sidewalk. Pocketing it quick, his shoes scraped the pavement as he stormed back toward the restaurant.

Prairie clutched her now naked neckline, the tears coming strong. She wanted to pretend it wasn't happening, but Billy had changed more than she wanted to believe. That kind, gentle side was his mask to whatever cruel and disrespectful monster he had become. She never thought he'd drift so far. Maybe she pushed too hard. Maybe she should have given in sooner and then she could have stopped this.

"You all right?" Marrok's calm voice overtook her attention. She looked up, seeing he was closer and offering her his handkerchief.

"Oh, thank you." She took it and lightly dabbed under her eyes. It was soft and smelled of fresh linen brought in from the line. She handed it back to him, but he didn't take it.

"You hold on to it."

"No. I couldn't."

"I insist."

She gave a weak smile before tucking it into her bag.

Marrok removed his hat, holding it gingerly to his chest. "If there's anything I can do."

"I'll be fine." With a deep sigh she flashed a forced smile his way. "You're making a habit of rescuing me."

He shook his head with a slight sense of doubt reflecting in those soft browns of his, "You were handling him just fine."

Prairie pressed her hands into the belt around her waist, letting out the last of her tension in a short breath, "What are you doing here anyway?"

He was quiet, letting the silence take over the conversation. Prairie waited, studying his gaze. He kept his focus to the ground, returning his hat to his head. Reaching into his pocket, he pulled out a card of matches. "Just on my way somewhere."

"I see." Prairie watched him light up, taking a long drag on his cigarette, looking up into the sky like it would give him some kind of answer. She fumbled with her bag. "Well, thank you again."

The ground crunched beneath her flats as she turned slowly toward the bus depot. She wasn't even sure buses were running this late, but she could at least call a cab if she needed to.

"You got somewhere to be?" Marrok's question stopped her in her tracks. Prairie turned around, still keeping her bag close to her belt.

"Just home. I think I've had enough for one birthday."

"Today's your birthday?"

Nerves rattled her stomach for a quick minute. "That's why I was out. Billy was . . . taking me out."

Marrok's shoes slid on the sidewalk as he stopped in front of her. "I can take you home if you'd like. There's just somewhere I need to be first. If you don't mind stopping for a bit."

Prairie shook her head. "Oh, no. I don't want to disrupt your plans."

"Ain't no trouble."

"It's not your responsibility—"

"I don't mind. That is, if you don't mind me asking." The corner of his lips peaked, showing off that cool grin that made her heart swoon and her breath fall short.

Prairie waited like the answer she already knew she was going to give would speak for her. Despite his tie being undone, he looked sharp and tasteful. But there was no shaking that uneasiness he was trying to hide. Each time she saw him, it seemed to be harder and harder for him to keep it in. Prairie could feel her legs shake from how badly she wanted to go with him. She shouldn't want to go with him.

"I . . . I don't mind." She said almost blissfully.

"Does that mean yes?"

He sounded playful, like he was getting a rise out of dragging out them standing alone on the street, with nothing but the buzz of the streetlamps to share the night. Prairie held her breath, pressing her fingers into the handle of her bag.

"Do you . . . want me to come with you?" The question eased off her tongue. It was bold, even for her. Bold because no girl in their right mind would ask such a question of a colored man. They weren't allowed to even suggest fancying a girl like her, outside the lines of what society deemed appropriate. But she needed to know if he was just being nice or if these chance meetings were less by chance.

Marrok's smile grew, stretching out his scar and flashing his teeth for a breath. "If you're askin' if I enjoy your company, then yes." His chin tilted down, like he needed to catch himself, before he came back to meet her gaze. "Very much so."

The sudden stampede of her heart squeezed her lungs. Prairie bit her tongue, relaxing her shoulders with another exhale. To hear those words, that he enjoyed being with her as much as she enjoyed being with him, it opened the doors of her heart even more, waiting for him to take the final step. "Where's your car?"

Chapter 13
The Jazz

They arrived at a line of old buildings. Music leaked from the stairs descending from the street. Marrok took the lead, Prairie just a step behind him. The farther down they went, the louder the music. There were drums and a bass playing with the shrill buzz of a saxophone. This was jazz, so alive it sent her heart dancing.

Marrok got to the door. It was thick with deep rooted bolts like a meat locker would have. A slot at the top was closed tight, keeping the music that already seeped from the cracks of the door from escaping much more. Marrok raised his hand and tapped on the surface. Prairie wasn't sure if anyone would hear them, but the slot opened suddenly to a pair of eyes peering out.

"My God." The man on the other side spoke. He closed the slot quickly before the door shifted open. A tall colored man with buzzed hair, wearing dark pressed slacks, a blazer and tie, stepped from the doorway. He had a peppered face, making her think he was around the same age as her daddy.

His hand was extended with a joyful expression. "Mad Dog." He breathed as Marrok took his hand. "It's been a while."

"Too long, Dick." Marrok pulled him into a hearty embrace. Prairie watched them patiently, not wanting to draw attention to herself.

"Well, it's great to see you, old friend." Dick glanced over to her, dark eyes lighting up. "And who is this?"

Prairie did the polite thing and lowered herself in a subtle curtsey. "Pleased to meet you. My name is Prairie O'Shea."

"She's with me." Marrok looked at her, flashing his classy smooth coated grin. "A friend."

"Well." Dick bowed graciously to her. "Any friend of Mad Dog is welcome here." He stepped back inside, ushering them in. "Come on in. The music's fine tonight."

Without asking, Marrok took her hand in his. The moment her fingers slipped into his palm, Prairie couldn't quite remember how to breathe. Her eyes wouldn't stray from their connection as he led her into the club. Once the intensity of the saxophone struck her ears, she was able to draw away.

It was a jazz club. A bar lined the entire east side. Buckets of seats held colored patrons sipping on glasses and enjoying a laugh. Small round tables and chairs were scattered on either side of the large domed dance floor, where dresses swung, and smoke billowed into the air.

Prairie ducked her head, keeping close to Marrok as other people came up to greet him with warm smiles and generous hands. When their eyes found her, she couldn't help but feel like a duck out of water. There wasn't anybody like her in this place. She was the only white person here.

Marrok led her to an empty table, pulling her toward the seat. "I gotta take care of something." He waited for Prairie to sit before relinquishing her hand. "Can I get you anything?"

"No, I'm fine." Prairie forced a smile, feeling smaller by the minute.

He placed his hat on the table. "I won't be long."

He slipped into the crowd, swallowed up so quickly, Prairie couldn't tell where he'd gone. She tucked her legs underneath the table, slipping her hands in her lap and keeping her eyes trained on the candle flickering in the center. She didn't need to see how many people were looking at her, wondering what a white girl was doing in a place like this. Prairie tried to ignore the feeling of being a caged animal. She never felt so exposed before. So vulnerable.

What was she even doing here? She promised both her folks and Beverly that she would be more careful. Yet here she was, not being careful at all. She didn't even know where *here* was. She'd never been to this part of town before. How would she even get home without Marrok?

Marrok. It was so easy to get lost with him. And when he was standing right in front of her, she barely had the will to resist. It was almost impossible. She wasn't acting like herself, and yet, she never felt more herself at the same time. Like she didn't have to pretend everything was made in the shade. All the messy things seem so normal when she was with him. More real.

"Hey there!" A sweet-faced colored girl in a sassy green swing dress pulled the seat from across the table and sat down. She looked young, maybe a few years younger than Prairie, but nothing more. "What's your name, honey?"

Prairie looked at her, tracing the lines of her angled profile and pulled back hair. She had beautiful light brown skin. "Oh, hello." Prairie smiled. "My name's Prairie."

"I'm Fiona." She reached over the table and took her hand, shaking it gingerly but not at all bothered about who she was engaging with. "Nice to make your acquaintance, Prairie."

"You as well." The uneasy feeling began to melt away. "Your name is lovely."

"Why thank you." Fiona gave a cheeky grin. "It's a family name." She looked into the crowd, noticing Prairie's nervous posture. "Don't let them get to you. It's not every day a white girl comes 'round here."

"I suppose not."

"You came with Mad Dog." She leaned back in the seat. "Don't think I've ever seen him bring a girl here."

Prairie brought her hands to the table. "You know him?"

Fiona nodded. "Since I was a child. Though I haven't seen him in years. Not since he gave the club to my daddy to run on his own."

"Your daddy is Dick?" Prairie asked.

Fiona nodded. "Sure is. This used to be Mad Dog's place back in the day, but my daddy became part owner some odd years ago. Though Mad Dog never seems to get older. Always looks the same. Wonder what his secret is?"

His secret. There was so much about Marrok that seemed to fit into that one simple word. Like his strength, holding Billy back like he was nothing but a little kid, or that glint in his eyes. Maybe she was overthinking it, but something wasn't right. What Fiona had just said about him only deepened the mystery.

Clearing her throat in case getting lost in her head showed, she folded her arms on the table in front of her. "Why do you call him Mad Dog?"

Fiona shrugged. "Don't know. That's just what we call him. I don't even know his real name."

The band started up again with a new number. Prairie turned toward the stage as it lit up with sounds and movement that electrified the dance floor. "This place is swinging."

"Usually is." Prairie felt Fiona's eyes on her. She turned slowly to catch them. "Sorry."

Fiona smiled. "Just, you're the prettiest thing. I wish I could have freckles like you."

"That's kind of you to say." She said as she tucked back her ironed curls.

"And so polite, too. Not every day a white girl is so polite to the likes of me."

"Well, you came and sat with me. Seeing how nervous I was. I appreciate that."

Fiona leaned into her elbow. "I take it you ain't nervous anymore?"

Prairie smiled as she shook her head. "Not much."

"Good." Fiona placed her hand on Prairie's. "Don't worry your head, honey. You came with Mad Dog. Nobody can touch you here, and nobody will give you lip neither."

"Fiona!" Both their heads turned toward the bar. The bartender waved her over. "Got a call."

Fiona sighed, "Must be my white knight." She giggled and turned to Prairie before standing. "If you'll excuse me. Don't want to keep my beau waiting."

"It was lovely to meet you, Fiona."

"Likewise, Prairie." Fiona held out her hand again, which Prairie grasped warmly. "Maybe I'll see you again sometime."

"I'd like that. I work at the diner on 43, if you ever come by."

"Thank you, I'll remember that." Fiona let go and backed away. "Enjoy yourself now."

Fiona skipped merrily toward the back of the bustling club, her movement wafting the smoke in the air. Prairie sat quietly, looking over the crowd to see if she could spot Marrok, but he was nowhere to be seen. Fiona's innocent conversation played over and over in her head.

Marrok didn't look much older than her. Maybe 24 at the oldest, but Fiona said she knew him when she was a girl. Girl, meaning younger than 24, and he owned this place before then? That would make him much older than she thought he was.

And how did nobody know his real name? Maybe it was just Fiona, but Dick called him Mad Dog as well and they seemed close. Close enough that Marrok would make him part owner of this place.

There were more questions than answers surrounding this drifter who was slowly taking her breath away. Nothing made a lick of sense. The pages of this mystery grew longer and longer every time she was with him.

"You doin' all right?" Marrok's low voice turned her head, and she found him crouching down to her from behind her chair.

She looked up with a slight nod. "I'm all right."

"I'm almost done here, but there's one last thing that needs my attention." He came to stand beside her and offered her his hand. "Will you come with me?"

Prairie watched him as butterflies tickled the edges of her stomach. She raised her hand and slipped it into his soft, velvety touch. They whipped up something terrible, shivering her skin and pumping her heart through the spaces of her ribcage. "Okay."

He pulled her to her feet, holding her fingers tight as he led her through the crowd. Heads turned as she ducked between the patrons toward the stage. The uneasy feeling came back stronger now that they passed so close to her.

This place was for them. Not for her. She tried to ignore them, knowing that curiosity could get the better of anyone, no matter their skin. But not knowing what they felt seeing her hand in hand with a man many clearly respected, would make anyone uneasy in a sea not meant for her to cast into.

Dick took the microphone, his sharp suit catching the edges of light from the stage. "How y'all doing tonight, guys and dolls?" The crowd threw up an applause as Marrok stopped at the stage steps.

"Just taking a minute to welcome back a man who needs no introduction. My friend. My brother." Dick turned to him, extending his hand. "The Mad Dog is back, ladies and gentlemen."

Dick barely finished his sentence before the crowd overtook him with whistles and shouts too loud for Prairie to distinguish a single word spoken. Dropping her hand, Marrok took to the stage, waving to the crowd with a smile as Dick grabbed him for another hug.

Prairie couldn't help but smile at the effect this so-called drifter had on this place. He was important to them. A man granted so much love, she wished she had been there when it was first bestowed. Marrok wasn't the least bit rattled by the reception; like he'd done it so many times before. Despite her still not knowing much about him, he was clearly a man with good intentions and a heart to match.

"Thank you, so much. I . . . I'm truly humbled by each and every one y'all." Marrok spoke and the crowd immediately died down.

"I am so pleased to see that Dick has done so well." He turned toward his friend. "Just as I knew he would." Dick laughed, placing a hand on Marrok's shoulder before stepping off to give him the stage.

"But there's others still out there that need this. And I aim to give'm the opportunity to find their place. A place of love. To nourish each other. Like y'all do here." The entire club roared like thunder. It hit Prairie square in the gut, filling her with the love Marrok spoke of just moments before. She could only join in their applause, smiling up at Marrok as he looked at her.

This was the most comfortable she had seen him since he stepped into the diner. He was home here, able to let his guard down, and just enjoy being alive. It was refreshing to see him show off his true colors, and it only validated that she was right about him.

A man this revered and loved by others couldn't be a murderer.

The room died down again as he continued. "I'd be lying if I said it was perfect, but there are some—" Prairie's eyes grew. "Some that want it as much as we do."

He raised his hand toward her and faced the people. "I have a very special someone with me tonight. Believe me when I say, she's got the voice of a songbird and a heart to match."

Marrok's sweet brown eyes found her again. "Miss. Prairie O'Shea."

Chapter 14
The Stage

Prairie opened her mouth, but no words fell out. She clutched onto the blue billow of her dress, moving the fabric between her fingers. Marrok turned back to the crowd. "Y'all want to hear her sing?"

They joined him in his request, with applause and shouts of encouragement, but nothing could stop her bones from shaking.

What was he doing? Prairie backed away, nerves forcing her to look at the floor, hoping nobody could see her.

But Marrok came down from the stage. "Since when are you the bashful type, Miss. Prairie?"

Prairie looked at him and shook her head. "I ain't cut out for this. I'm not going up there."

"You got the jitters is all." With the gentlest care, he took her hand. Prairie looked into his eyes, and a calming warmth washed over her from the tips of her fingers to the bottom of her toes. "I'll be watching you, right here." He gestured toward the wall by the stairs. "Keep your eyes on me for as long as you need."

Prairie forgot how to breathe, but the next one she took shook the jitters clear from her.

"Why are you doing this?" She asked softly enough so that only he could hear.

"Giving you a chance. A chance to show the world we ain't so different. To see it is something rare. Something beautiful."

She couldn't stop herself from being in awe of him. "What kind of man are you, Marrok?"

Nerves littered his breath. She could tell he wasn't used to this, letting someone into this part of his life. Someone like her. "I'm just a man. Like any other."

"You're not like any man I've ever known."

"Well, you ain't like any girl I've ever known either, Miss. Prairie." He looked toward the stage. "You ready?"

Prairie held the air in her lungs and nodded. The next few steps, he let her go as her feet graced the stage. The crowd continued to clap as she curtsied with her hands on the blue of her dress. She grasped the mic carefully, her palms still slightly slick with nerves.

"Hello." She spoke into the mic with surprising shyness. "My name is Prairie O'Shea." Her gaze flashed to Marrok. He stood against the wall, arms folded, still looking back at her.

"I'm a . . . waitress at the Moonlight Diner on 43." She looked back out, the blaring lights finally bringing things into focus. "I'm sure I've served some of you before. If you fancy peach pie and a cup of coffee at two in the morning."

A few laughs met the smoke of the room.

"Anyway." She looked at her feet. "Guess I better sing for you now." She turned toward the band behind her.

"What's your pleasure, ma'am?" The blue-tuxed bassist asked.

"Give me a beat." She said, "I'll just feel for something, I suppose." She stifled a breath.

"I've never done this before."

"There's a first time for everything, ma'am." The bassist smiled, as his fingers started to pluck at the strings.

Prairie turned and caught Marrok's eyes again, holding onto them as she felt the music seep into her feet. Her fingers dropped, snapping along to the tempo as a familiar song came to mind. Marrok watching her was all she needed to let her voice sail through the mic, projecting a fever over the crowd.

Drums kept the time. The sax battling down the notes left and right. Every word sung was more confident than the next. It wasn't long before she didn't need to see Marrok watching her for her eyes to close, taking the microphone like it was a part of who she was.

The feeling was like nothing else. Except perhaps when Marrok held her hand. So high, without fearing the fall.

Chapter 15
The Dance

The applause didn't start to die until she was off the stage, elated at a performance well received. She never felt so full, like a cup aching to breach the edge. Marrok still clung to the wall, arms folded with a grin.

Prairie strolled over to him, her arms swinging as the band started playing again.

"Satisfied?"

"Like I said, you're a natural."

"I haven't felt this good in a long time." She settled in beside him, leaning back against the wall. "I have you to thank for that."

Marrok followed her, holding on to that smile. "That right?"

"Thank you."

He kept his gaze on her. Prairie matched his smile, tilting her head against the wall before playfully rolling her shoulders to come off it. "What's the matter? Cat got your tongue?"

"Something like that."

The last song started to wind down, with both of them unable to leave the other. Prairie's pulse rushed to her head, creating a warmth inside her she couldn't quite place. Everything sounded muffled from how loudly her heart was beating.

"And now, for all you lovers out there." The voice from the

stage echoed as the band started up again, smoothing out the tone as it crawled through the smoke-filled room.

Prairie turned toward the crowd, watching the song lull the dancers into a closeness as the sax carried them in their stride.

"May I?"

Marrok's presented his hand to her. She looked at it before finding his gaze. With a smile, she laced her fingers in his as he led her onto the floor. Wrapping his arm around her waist, their hands remained entwined as the other fell against his chest. She was almost afraid to look up. There wasn't a part of her that wasn't tingling all over. Her heart beat like a drum, feeling his steady rhythm through her fingertips.

Some watched them together, unreadable in their blank expressions. Most people didn't fancy seeing a white girl sweeping the dance floor with a colored man, even after she entertained them with her song. It wasn't natural.

The thought must have been written all over her face. Marrok touched her chin to draw her attention. "If this is botherin' you . . ."

When she was brave enough to fall on his baby browns, he smiled that warm, almost mischievous grin that pulled one just like it across her freckled cheeks. "I rather enjoy you bothering me."

He pulled her closer, letting the wall of his musky forest scent fill her lungs. A sudden urge began to take hold. She was sure her palms were sweating, but he didn't even bat an eye.

Kissing a colored man, the thought never crossed her mind, but that was before Marrok came waltzing into her diner with his slick boots and inescapable grin. Her daddy taught her that everyone deserves to be treated with kindness and respect, no matter their class or color. But that was before this. Before his plump, full lips hung mere inches from her face.

It wasn't taboo, why even think it was such a thing? But society was cruel. No one would understand how this colored man, with a scar on his face, swept her off her feet, and less understanding wouldn't give her the chance to breath a word about it.

As the song wound down, the crowd began their applause, but Prairie couldn't let go. They stood together, lost in the whistles and roars of their fellow patrons. It was surreal how different this felt from when she was with Billy just a few hours before. Nostalgia was carrying her then, in their words and actions: an innocent hope. But this, this was laced with more than she was expecting. A longing that sat so heavy between them, she wanted to buckle from the weight of it.

Praying that his arms would carry her to some far-off place where it could just be them.

When he leaned forward, Prairie's heart leapt into her throat. He wouldn't dare kiss her now. Not here. As much as the thought sent her heart charging down an endless highway, with no hope of stopping.

He touched his cheek to hers, mouth nestled in her ear. "I hope I'm not being too forward. But you're shining tonight. A star pulled from the sky."

Prairie's freckles popped hot across her cheeks as he pulled away, tucking a strand of her cherry brown hair gingerly behind her ear.

"It's gettin' late. Best get you home now."

He peeled away from her, except for his hand. They stayed locked together, as he led her from the dance floor. No amount of breathing could calm the sputtering of her heart. The muffled sounds of voices tried to get her head on straight, but she was spinning. Spinning so fast she thought she'd come right off the ground.

Chapter 16
The Truth

The car hummed quietly down the open road. It was pretty bare, only one or two neighboring headlights gracing the windshield as they drove. The moon was full and clear, peeking in from the side window every time Prairie tilted her head against the glass.

They came around a bend and Prairie sat up from the seat. "Can we stop here?"

Marrok didn't object, pulling their ride over and cutting the engine. Prairie opened the door and stepped out into the night. She rushed up the hill in front of her, holding her dress so it wouldn't touch down on any dampness that may be lingering in the tall grass.

When she got to the top, she stopped and gazed up into the sky. The moon was as bright as the sun. Lines of clouds touched its face, caressing it as they passed, traveling into the darkness.

She sighed, letting her shoulders drop and hands come to rest at her sides. Marrok approached slowly, taking a step in beside her, dropping his jacket over her shoulders.

"It's beautiful, isn't it?" She asked with her eyes still trained to the sky.

"Yeah. Beautiful."

She turned to him; his attention carefully placed on her. His sleeves were rolled up to his elbows. Gray suspenders ran up across his shoulders. A few more buttons were open on his shirt, exposing the train of his neck.

Prairie pulled his jacket to cover more of her arms. The moonlight kissed his face, bringing his scar to the forefront of her gaze. "I hope you don't mind me asking . . ."

"Bout what?"

She motioned to her face. "Your scar."

Marrok shook his head. "That's a story not fit for a girl like you."

"A girl like *me*?" She grinned, leaning on her right leg. "And here I thought you knew what kind of girl I was."

When he didn't respond, Prairie shook her head, realizing that she had no right to pry. "I'm sorry. Ignore my nosey self. I don't know when to mind my own business."

The cool air laced through the loose strands of her hair. Marrok hesitated, his eyes shifting in indecisiveness.

"I was shot."

Prairie's muscles tensed. "You were . . . shot?"

He nodded slowly, finally taking a chance to look at her. "When I was 12. My family had a farm in West Virginia. We were given the land and worked it freely. Made a livin'. But not without paying our dues to the local . . . enforcement."

His gaze shifted, trailing toward the ground before climbing into the sky. Prairie practically held her breath as she waited for him to continue his story, knowing it wouldn't have a happy ending.

"Crop was bad one year. We didn't have enough to give 'em. Not without sacrificing for ourselves." He shook his head. "They didn't take kindly to that. They came one night. Barreling through the kitchen. Whippin' their pistols in the air like it was their right to use 'em. They came, tried to take my sisters. Gutted my mama like a pig to get 'em."

Prairie raised her hand to her mouth, eyes too terrified to blink.

"Shot my pa. Dead before he hit the floor." Marrok didn't take his eyes from the sky, as if his folks were up there, listening to him tell the story of how they died.

"My brothers chased them out the door. I was so scared; I could barely move from under the table. I heard fightin'. I knew I had to try to do something. So, I got to the door . . . just in time to see them cut down my brothers. Stabbed and shot them in the back."

"They dragged my sisters to their truck by their hair. They were screamin' so loud . . . sometimes I can still hear them." He folded his hands in front of him, looking down at his fumbling fingers.

"That's when they came for me. They caught me. Dragged me by my legs and kicked in my stomach. I can still feel the cold barrel of the gun on my face. They shot me so fast . . . I barely heard the bullet leave the barrel before hitting the ground."

Prairie's breath caught in her throat. She swallowed, shutting her eyes to the terrible events Marrok had laid out in the night. "I . . . I don't know what to say. People can be so cruel . . ."

She looked at Marrok, his gaze cutting through the night.

"Not all people." He came back, eyes shifting from the memories.

Prairie could not imagine how scared he must have been. How much hurt and pain he had to endure in those moments and all that came after. "How did you get away?"

He took a deep breath, nostrils flaring as he exhaled. "Somebody came. Ran them off. Took me in. Helped me heal. Got me together and taught me how to see the good in the world again. And how I could be part of that good."

"Where are they now?"

"Dead." He spoke so plainly, it sent shivers down her spine, "That is, he left one night. Never came back."

"And your sisters?"

Marrok hesitated, shifting in his stance. "I found them again. After a time. But I couldn't stay with them."

She tightened her grip on his jacket. "Why not?"

"Truth is." He looked down at his unsettled hands. "Who I was before, that boy with a bullet in his head. I can never become who that boy was supposed to be."

They waited, letting the crickets become the chorus of their thoughts. Prairie had never heard a sadder song. Knowing how horrid the world was that it destroyed a boy's family just because some men thought themselves superior. It weighed on her soul, so heavy she thought she'd fall.

How could God allow such injustice to befall those he claimed to love?

But maybe it was people like Marrok that He sent to make things right. Even though she still didn't fully understand. Marrok was someone people respected and admired, but he was still a mystery created from a tragedy no one could crawl back from without the strength to do so.

"Mind if I say something?" Prairie spoke calmly as Marrok looked at her.

"Course not."

She took a short breath, turning herself toward him. "I don't want to diminish the terrible acts brought down on your family. I think those men should burn for what they'd done to you and your own. No one deserves what happened to you, and it pains my heart to think of how you must have suffered."

The corner of his mouth cracked. "You don't need to be sorry, but I appreciate you sayin' so."

She flashed a weak smile, before tilting her head down slightly. "I . . . can't help but be a little grateful."

He furrowed his brow. "Grateful?"

Prairie held her breath, hoping her next words wouldn't come across as distasteful. "Where you came from. What happened to you. It made you who you are. It brought you to my diner at 2 A.M. on a Tuesday morning." Marrok turned to face her. "There's something I can't shake since meeting you. Something I've read that keeps coming back each time I find myself looking at you."

She blinked as he held her focus. "Any coincidence is always worth noticing. You can throw it away later if it is only a coincidence." She lightly shook her head. "This isn't that. It's never been just a . . . coincidence."

Marrok took a step, tracing his fingers across her cheek and coming to rest at the back of her hairline. Bells rang in her ears from his touch and his forest dew perfume stirred her mind.

She grasped his wrist, feeling slightly light-headed from him being so close to her. Color be damned; a man was a man, and she never thought she'd meet a man like him. Maybe she didn't know it when his boots sat at the counter that night, but she knew now just how much that wanting never stopped. Wanting to know everything there was to know about him. To be part of whatever he was here to do, even if it were dangerous. She couldn't say no to it. Not the fear and exhilaration that melted together whenever she was around him.

"Miss. Prairie," he swallowed, his mouth coming apart mere centimeters from her own.

"How many times do I have to tell you not to call me miss." Her voice was but a whisper as he inched ever closer.

A hint of tobacco leaked from his breath onto her face. Goose pimples ran up her arms and legs, sending her senses tingling and her pulse racing like mad. Her hand met his face, cupping the scar and feeling it rise from his darkened skin. He flinched, momentarily taking him out of the moment. They studied one another, each yearning for something, though Prairie could only hope what that was, was one in the same.

Marrok's gaze left her face, his fingers falling from the back of her neck. "We can't do this."

Prairie's stomach twisted into a painful knot, causing her lungs to ache. "I didn't think anything could scare you."

"You don't understand," he lowered his hand to clutch onto hers, keeping it between them. She watched his thumb rub over the top of her knuckles, leaving remnants of his wants across the tops of her fingers. "I can't be selfish."

Prairie's lips folded. It felt right, but at the same time, it was wrong. Wrong according to what kind of fella a girl like her should be wanting. But nothing about this felt like she was breaking any creeds. If God loved everyone equally, why would He forbid this?

His pulse radiating against her skin like it belonged. But maybe it was too much to risk, even for him. She needed to know if he was feeling all this like she was.

"Does it feel wrong?"

Marrok looked at her. He wasn't holding anything back anymore. Nothing was there to thwart her, only his soul looking straight back into hers.

"No, it don't." He took a step to the left keeping her hand in his, "Come on, I've kept you here long enough."

Marrok led her to the car, opening the door for her to get in. Prairie sunk into the seat, heavy with everything that was running through her head. She kept her hands folded in her lap, still feeling his thumb on her skin.

Marrok got into the driver's seat and put the key in the ignition. The car purred to life as he reached for the clutch. She shot out her hand, landing right on top of his. He looked at her, that cool expression knotted with disappointment. She wasn't sure if it was for her or himself. Maybe it was both.

But it doesn't feel wrong, she thought, *so it must be right. It's got to be.*

Slowly, she drew away from him and focused on the beam of the headlights. Marrok pulled back onto the road, illuminating their way home. Prairie watched them pass over the dark pavement, lighting a path that was always there, even when there were no cars to reveal it existed.

In a lot of ways, she was seeing things for the first time, too. Things that were always present, and yet constantly overlooked. A nagging question grew louder and louder the longer she sat in the fine leather seats of Marrok's Thunderbird.

Why couldn't this be right?

Chapter 17
The Escape

The car ride home seemed like it went on forever. Prairie leaned back in the seat, keeping her eyes on Marrok's hand resting on the stick. She observed every line and fold, wondering what they'd held or kept at some point in his life. Guess it didn't matter now. The only thing she wanted them to hold was her.

Marrok looked at her, his jaw still holding on to all manner of regret of whatever it was that he was keeping himself from doing. Prairie couldn't hold it against him, but she hoped that maybe that wasn't important enough to get in the way. She had a feeling though, deep down in her gut, that it was more than just a matter of skin.

"You won't see me again after tonight."

Marrok's cold tone tied her up inside. She clutched her arms to her chest, tightening her lips to keep her emotions from spilling out, "Is that cuz you don't want to see me?"

"No."

The weight lifted off Prairie's face from that single word. His lips puckered, narrowing his eyes to the road with a harsh exhale that flared his nostrils like a bull.

"I'm bad news," he glanced at her, moving both hands to the wheel. "People get hurt knowing me like you do."

"Dick seemed to know you better than I do," she lowered her arms. "Is it okay for him to know you and not me?"

"That's different."

"You don't need to keep quiet," she huffed, wanting to find the truth to his reasons. "It's because I don't look like them, right?"

His hands came off the wheel and slammed down, widening her eyes with a start. "God damn it, Prairie," he growled. "You don't know nothin' so stop pretendin' that you do."

Her pulse quickened to the rising tension that slowly took over the cab. "What I do," he continued, aggressively stabbing himself in the chest with his finger, "it ain't worth getting mixed up in."

There was some idea in her head of the *'what'* and *'why'* surrounding Marrok, but that fact didn't stop him from talking to her or getting in the way every time Billy seemed to raise a hand in her direction. Her disappointment started to mount into quickening anger. This situation wasn't something she could control.

"Then why did you invite me to come with you," her chest tightened as she came off the seat. "Why'd you bring me to that place and dance with me? You could have just let me deal with Billy, but you stepped in. *Why?* You walked into my business and got this stirred up from the second you came into my diner. It was—"

"It was a mistake."

He might as well have slapped her in the face. Prairie shrunk back into the seat, digging her teeth into her bottom lip, hoping it would hurt more than his words. Marrok's chest heaved, holding his breath as he stared unblinking at the road in front of them.

"Just a selfish mistake." His eyes dropped as he exhaled, looking her way but not meeting her eyes, "I'm sorry."

Prairie turned, staring out the passenger side window. She wiped a stray tear from her face, trying like mad not to break right here in this car.

Was he playing with her this whole time? No, it didn't feel that way. He could have been flirty and forward if he wanted to, but he wasn't. He talked to her like she had an opinion and ideas that mattered. Like she wasn't just a girl with her head in the clouds, as Billy would say.

Maybe it was because most colored folks knew to respect and act polite around white folks. But they wouldn't give them a ride home, or sneak into a diner to talk to them, or take them to a club for a dance. Or almost kiss them in the moonlight.

Her eyes pressed, allowing another bead of sadness to fall before wiping her freckled cheeks clean of any evidence of how much this was hurting.

"Not as sorry as I am," she breathed.

She just wanted to be home, be alone in her room, hugging her pillow to her chest as she dreamed of what this night could have been. With Billy or with Marrok, but she was used to Billy disappointing her. She didn't expect it from Marrok, but then again, she didn't even know who this man really was.

Prairie kept her eyes on the dark forest surrounding the highway before Marrok veered down an exit. Soon, homes and fenced in yards echoed in the streetlamps of the residential part of Oak Springs.

Just a little longer, and she could forget this night ever happened. But she didn't want it to end. Not like this. Not wounded from something that never was anything to begin with. Or maybe it was something . . . something unwanted by others, but not by her.

"You can do anythin' you set your mind to, Prairie."

She gently rolled against the headrest to meet Marrok's gaze. He no longer seemed tense, but there was still that mild regret leaking from his eyes as he looked at her. "Don't let someone like me get in your way."

She forced a smile, but only for a second. It was an excuse. As if his belief in her was so strong he was willing to step aside and not stand in the way of her dreams. He was preventing them from crossing the line they were about to cross. The fact that it even strayed to her mind should be enough of a warning, but it didn't cause as much fear as she thought it would. There was hardly any fear at all. Only yearning.

"Sure," tumbled from her mouth. A defeated word for a defeated situation. This was the end of it. She wanted to believe he wasn't telling the truth when he said she wouldn't see him again. It was the truth and that was what hurt most of all.

Before Prairie could turn her gaze from Marrok's, he laid heavy on the brake. They both lurched forward, coming to a complete stop. Prairie caught her breath, looking through her disheveled hair to find a girl running toward the car headlights.

Tears wet her light brown face and her sassy, green dress was tarnished with dirt and ripped up to the waist. Prairie's eyes narrowed before they sprung to life. Without a word, she ran from the car as the girl reached the hood, Marrok not too far behind.

"Fiona." Prairie caught her as she fell into her arms. "God in heaven, what happened?"

"A man!" Fiona pointed toward the forest. "A man . . . he was . . . trying to kidnap me. I was . . . oh, Lord . . . he had a gun!"

"Take a deep breath." Prairie cradled her and looked at Marrok, who stood with his jaw clenched and his nostrils flaring.

"Where'd you come from?" He asked with determination.

Fiona turned to him and clenched her fists. "I ran. For a long time." She pointed to the forest again. "I don't know how far, but on the other side o' here."

Marrok's stare moved toward the dark trees standing in the still night.

"Stay here." And he moved, so fast, Prairie barely had time to react.

"Wait." She let go of Fiona and followed his determined stride. "Where are you going?"

"Stay here an' if I don't come back in 5 minutes," He handed her his keys, "take my car n' drive on home."

"That doesn't answer my question, Marrok." She grabbed his arm, spinning him around.

"Where are you going?"

Marrok's eyes caught the light of the moon as it hung in the sky. Not a shift or blink kept his gaze from her. Prairie tried to stand firm, but there was something different lingering in his eyes. Something she never saw before.

"Don't follow me." He didn't need much to get his arm back from her. Prairie watched him walk into the forest, leaving her and Fiona standing in the running headlights of his dark Thunderbird. He looked mean. Like how he was when she saw him beating on the man at the drive-in. Mean and ready for a fight.

Fiona ran to her side, gazing out into the undisturbed treeline like someone didn't pass through mere moments ago.

"Where's he going?"

"I don't know." Prairie pulled Marrok's jacket tighter around her. Something didn't feel right. Something was wrong and Marrok running clear into it didn't help ease the shifting in her stomach. She turned to Fiona, fussing over her sullied self. "You aren't hurt, are you?"

"No." Fiona shook her head. "Maybe a few bumps and bruises, but I'll be all right."

Prairie rubbed her shoulders, seeing her shivering from the chill or perhaps shock of the ordeal. "You're cold." She relinquished Marrok's jacket and threw it around Fiona's shoulders.

"Thank you." She smiled weakly.

"The man who was trying to take you. What did he look like?"

Fiona swallowed. "I didn't get a good look at him, but he wasn't my date. He was . . . a stranger."

Prairie recalled the club, remembering Fiona saying something about meeting up with a fella of hers. Her white knight.

"Did something happen to the boy you were with?" She continued to rub her shoulders to try and stop Fiona from shivering.

"I . . . I don't know. One minute we were necking in his car. And the next . . . I was in someone else's car . . . with that—"

A shot rang through the trees and silenced their words. Both Fiona and Prairie looked toward the sky, seeing a few roused birds escape from the tops of them.

"Oh no." Fiona whispered.

The hair on the back of Prairie's neck started to tingle. Marrok was out there. He could be hurt, or worse.

Holding onto Fiona, she walked her to the car and sat her in the open door of the driver's seat. "You stay here. Don't leave the car." Prairie reached over her and placed the key in the ignition, turning it to start the engine. "You lock the doors and keep 'em tight."

Fiona grabbed Prairie by the arms. "You can't go out there. You can't!"

"I'll be right back." Fiona nestled into the seat as Prairie hung on the door. "Just . . . stay here. You'll be safe."

"Prairie."

But she had already closed the door, watching Fiona to make sure she locked it. After her fingers pushed the button, Fiona placed her hand on the window, which Prairie reciprocated. "I'll be back."

The uneasiness in her stomach kept her feet moving fast. She had to find Marrok.

Her heart was beating so fast she thought it might run ahead of her. Breaking through the trees, the branches whipped at her skin, pulling her hair, and stumbling her feet. She was going in blind. Nothing but the light of the moon and the sound of rustling leaves to guide her.

As she made her way in deeper, something caught her attention. Prairie stopped, crouching down next to a white shirt lying amongst the dead leaves. There wasn't an inch of dirt on it, aside from where it lay. It was Marrok's shirt. Picking it up, she clenched it in her fists as a faint rumble filtered through the trees.

With a steady approach, Prairie stepped toward the shifting of leaves and quiet splitting of branches. The closer the sounds came, the clearer they were. Like an animal. Wild and unhinged.

Her heart was clear in her mouth now, batting at the back of her teeth, forcing her legs to stop working. There wasn't enough air in her lungs as she parted the stray branches that shielded her from whatever creature was lurking in the shadows.

With a shaky hand, she laced her fingers through the leaves, pushing them aside to clear her view.

Chapter 18
The Wolf

A figure lay on the ground, lifeless and stagnant, except for the subtle movements caused by the dark mass bending over it.

A sudden whiff of wet dog tickled her nose as she brought her hand up to quell the strength of it. Moonlight parted the hair that covered its back and arms. Its ears were pointed, and a long wolf-like tail curved toward the treetops. As her eyes adjusted, she could see the face of a man the monster was tearing apart, vacant and frozen in the terror that had taken him.

Prairie gasped, stepping back into the branches.

The crunch from her footsteps drew the beasts' attention. Pointed fangs jutted from its narrow snout. Blood dripped from its mouth as it wiped across them with sharpened claws. It was big, bigger now that it was standing on two legs. There was not a scrap of flesh uncovered by a coat of thick, black fur. As Prairie's shifting eyes met its own, she saw something familiar.

That threatening glint across the same eyes she had lost herself in just a short while ago.

She couldn't hold onto Marrok's shirt tight enough, watching this creature, who stood like a man. But looked like a wolf.

She turned and ran without looking back. Still clutching the shirt to her chest, she broke through the trees, letting the fear sink

through her damp shoes. The dark Thunderbird purred with its lights blaring out onto the open road. Fiona saw her approach and flung the door open, stepping out of the car.

"What happened?" She gasped, keeping Marrok's jacket around her shoulders. "You look like you saw a ghost."

"We need to go." Prairie pushed past her. "I'll drive."

"Prairie, what's going on?"

"Prairie."

She turned to find Marrok emerging from the forest. He was covered in all matter of forest debris, blood and pieces of something she could only imagine were flesh. His slacks were on haphazardly, dirtied just as his chest was. Blood stained his fingers, still wet from the freshness of the kill. Prairie ignored him as she pushed Fiona back to the car, trying to outrun the truth of what she saw.

"What happened? Why does he got blood on his hands?" Fiona kept looking back at the state of Marrok, eyes wide with curiosity and misplaced fear.

"Get in the car, Fiona." Prairie continued to usher her past the headlights. Fiona obliged and opened the passenger side door, closing it and immediately locking herself inside.

Prairie kept her gaze on the ground as she moved around the car. Bare feet caught her eye against the pavement. A hand grabbed her arm, forcing her to find his. She yanked herself away, backing into the door with a thud.

"Get your hands off me!"

"I told you to stay here." His voice was forceful and stern.

"You don't control me! I do as I please." Prairie grasped the handle on the driver's side door.

"I just wanna explain . . ."

Her hair cut across her face as she whipped around to confront him. "There's *nothing* you can say to me!" Her chest heaved as silence passed between them.

It was hard to look at him, standing there like a lost puppy in the rain. Prairie couldn't put two and two together. She had no proof it was him, despite the look of his eyes. It matched the creature's so well you'd think they were plucked from his skull and handed to him on a silver platter.

His shirt was still clenched in her fist. Squeezing it to her chest, she threw it at him.

Marrok caught it, glancing down before meeting her again. "You best get out of here, Marrok."

His breathing was steady, the muscles of his arms flexed and poised. Prairie could feel herself unraveling, standing in the wake of a nightmare. She had to get away from him, if only to get her head on straight and figure out what this all meant.

"I'll leave the keys in the flap and park a few blocks from my house." She caught the fear drenched sorrow in her throat. "Get outta here!"

Without a second glance, she broke into the car, slamming the door. Fiona stared out the window as they carried down the road. Prairie couldn't stop her hands from shaking, no matter how hard she held the smooth surface of the wheel. They drove for longer than she needed to, going round in circles if only so Prairie had a chance to think.

"What are we gonna do now?" Fiona asked quietly.

Looking over at her passenger, Prairie saw a few extra tears leaking from her eyes. She was scared. Had every right to be. But nothing could fill a heart with more dreaded fear than what Prairie saw. Who she knew it to be.

"We're gonna park the car and go to my house." She glanced at the row of houses they were approaching. "You call your daddy to come get you. If my folks are awake, I'll just say you got lost is all. Needed help finding your way."

"What about Mad Dog?"

Prairie rolled their ride alongside the curb, cutting the engine. She turned toward Fiona, unable to focus on one particular answer, but Fiona took her hand and pressed her lips tight.

It was wrong not to tell someone what she saw. A man was ripped apart by a monster straight out of a horror flick. Who would believe it? Nobody. That's who. Nobody would believe her.

Fiona wouldn't say anything about it. She wanted to protect him because of what kind of man Marrok was. For what he did for her family. Prairie wanted to protect him from what he was hiding under his skin. Something so few probably even knew about. She had been swept off her feet by a man who wasn't exactly a man at all.

"Not a word." She squeezed Fiona's hand as her eyes glanced down at the bloody finger lines Marrok had left on her skin. "Not a word to nobody."

Chapter 19
The Questions

They sat in the kitchen by the phone with only the gentle hum of the fluorescent lights above to cut through the silence. Prairie paced barefoot across the black and white checkered floor, moving between the red refrigerator and the taupe-colored cabinets. Fiona had her hands on her lap, leg bouncing and mouth taut. Lorna and Jerry were sound asleep in their beds. Neither their arrival nor Fiona calling her daddy seemed to jar them awake.

Prairie kept looking at the clock, watching the minutes slowly creep from line to line.

"You think Mad Dog will find his car okay?" Fiona asked quietly, stopping Prairie in mid stride.

She looked at Fiona briefly, trying to sound calm but feeling all sorts of frantic. "Yeah. He'll find it just fine."

Marrok. What was he? She couldn't even be sure of what she saw and wondered if her mind was playing tricks on her. That towering, snarling monster with glinting teeth and sharp pointed ears. His hands and feet, like daggers encased in a bed of black fur. There was no denying those eyes. They were the same. Holding back in the calm serenity she longed for, behind a horrifying secret she wasn't supposed to see.

"Prairie?" Fiona stopped her again. This time, Prairie ceased

her stride. Her fingers pulled at themselves like a knot that she couldn't untie. "What did you see out there?"

The frightened girl in her wanted to scream the answer to anyone who was willing to listen. To not be alone in what she saw. It would make it more real. More true. But she couldn't bear to tell a soul. Not until she had a chance to talk to Marrok again and make sense of it all. "Nothing you need to worry about."

The sound of a car squeezing along the curb turned their heads. Both Prairie and Fiona quickly left the kitchen and crossed into the family room to the front door. Prairie opened it, seeing a shabby brown Ford parked, and Dick stepping up the path to the house.

Fiona ran into his arms, holding back tears through squinted eyes. Prairie walked down the three steps onto the cobblestone path and waited, hands still fiddling at her waist. Dick looked up at her, his eyes writing novels of truth without words.

Prairie followed them to the car, stepping in front to open the door so Fiona could get in. "Try and get some rest now." Fiona reached out and grasped Prairie's hand, nodding as tears streamed down her face.

"You'll be all right. I'll see you real soon." Prairie squeezed her hand, returning it to her lap before she quietly shut the door.

Dick came beside her, adjusting his fedora. "I can't thank you enough."

"No, I . . . I'm just glad she's okay."

They stood in an awkward silence. Prairie watched his mouth open and then close abruptly, like he was unsure of what to say. Words hung on the tip of her tongue, wanting to ask if he knew what Marrok was or anything that would help uncover the mystery surrounding him.

"Mad Dog . . ." He pressed his lips firmly before allowing himself to speak again. "Did he . . . is he—"

"He's okay." In her desperation for answers, she grasped his arm. "I . . . I saw . . . everything."

Dick watched her closely, lowering his tone. "I know ya have. I can see it in your eyes."

He held on to her, seeing the drag marks of blood Marrok left on her arm. "He ain't a monster."

A rush of cold wind washed over her. Like something you were begging for but regretted it the moment it hit your skin. What she saw was real. Terrifying and real. And if it was, what else could be? Blood sucking vampires? Cackling witches? Nothing made sense but explanations didn't matter at this point.

Prairie squeezed him before letting go. "You best get her home."

With a nod, he slid off the curb and dashed into the car. Prairie watched as they pulled away, the gentle pattering of the Ford slowly fading into the night.

She couldn't catch a wink. Each time she closed her eyes he was there. Dripping blood from his gnarled teeth and claws. She made a point to stay in bed until her folks left for the diner.

Even when she was alone, nothing could keep him from her thoughts.

When she finally readied for work, she walked down to the bus stop a few blocks from her home. Marrok's car was nowhere to be seen. Prairie wondered where he could have gone. If he skipped town or was still lurking in the shadows. When she reached the bus sign, she sat down on the bench, and placed her bag on her lap. Every car that drove past had her heart leaping into her throat thinking it was him. There was another woman, dressed in a white and black maid's outfit, her skin a smooth russet brown. She sat on another bench, marked 'colored,' eyes forward and back straight. Prairie stared at her, wondering if she knew Marrok too. Knew what he was or at least heard the name Mad Dog. The woman slowly turned to look at her, her eyes widening with a slightly disturbed expression.

Prairie turned away, trying to keep her thoughts from getting the better of her. After waiting a handful of time, a blue Desoto pulled up to the curb just before the bench. Prairie barely passed a glance, until she saw who got out of it.

Detective Greenway swung around the front wearing a trench coat with a plain gray suit, matching fedora, and red tie. "Good afternoon, Miss. O'Shea." He spoke while chewing on a stick.

Prairie watched him cautiously. "Good afternoon, Detective."

"Heading to work?"

She tightened her hold on her bag. "Yes, I am." She said with a single nod.

"Care for a lift?"

The hair on the back of her neck stood on end. He wasn't acting any different from the other times she'd spoken to him, but his tone suggested that he was aware of something. Something itching at him.

"Thank you, but—"

He took out his cigarette and blew smoke into the air. "There's something I wish to discuss with you. Regarding last night."

Prairie noticed the woman watching their exchange. She took a breath, her brow furrowed, trying to keep herself as cool as ice. "Don't you need a warrant or something to question me?"

"I prefer a good conversation. Off the record." He gestured toward his car. "If I may?"

Prairie sat in the car, knees plastered together, and hands folded in her lap. Her posture was straight as an arrow, keeping her eyes ahead, watching the lines on the road skip by one by one.

Greenway had both hands on the wheel. His hat tipped casually back to keep from disrupting his focus on the road. Every so often, he'd shake his smoke stick out the window to disperse the ashes. As they turned onto the highway, Prairie's pulse quickened in tandem with the speed of the car.

"A man was found last night." Greenway finally spoke. "Throat ripped clean open."

Prairie rolled her tongue along her gums before taking a breath. "And what does that have to do with me?"

"Maybe nothing. At least, I hope nothing. For your sake."

Prairie glanced at him, catching his dark eyed stare. Greenway's cig tapped the window's edge, before he brought it back between his lips. "I got a witness. Said they saw you arguing with someone on Willeston street in Oak Springs. William Hemsworth, I believe his name is."

"So?" Prairie forwarded her gaze. "Couples fight sometimes. It's not uncommon."

"Said they saw somebody step in. A colored man. With a scar on his face." Prairie's eyes hit the floor before trailing up toward the detective again. "And that you left with said colored man."

The car hit a bump or two, rocking Prairie in her seat. She kept herself firm, not knowing what she could say to diminish his suspicions. At this point, there wasn't any way she could, nor did she want to. But if this was all he knew—that a man was ripped apart on the same night she was with Marrok—then that is what she would leave him with.

The more they waited in silence, the more determined she was to keep it that way. "Did I commit a crime by doing so?"

Greenway adjusted his hands on the wheel. "So, you don't deny it?"

"No, sir. I'm not ashamed of it or got nothing to hide about it."

"Where did you go with him?"

She swallowed. "Nowhere."

"Did he take you home?"

"No sir."

"Then . . . he left . . . at some point after you were with him?"

She had to stop this line of questioning before the accounts of what happened started flooding out of her mouth. "That isn't any of your business."

He breathed in fiercely through his flaring nostrils. "You do understand the nature of this conversation, Miss. O'Shea."

"I understand it just fine." Prairie swallowed the hard lump forming in her throat. "What I don't understand is what a dead man has got to do with me or the company I keep."

Greenway snuffed his smoke in the ashtray underneath the radio . He raised a brow to Prairie, the corner of his mouth slightly raised. "The company you keep may not be who you think they are."

She held her breath, sucking in her stomach to keep it from folding over itself. "I think I can make that judgment for myself, Mr. Greenway."

He chuckled, breaking the rising tension. "You're a tough nut to crack, Miss. O'Shea. Ever think about joining law enforcement? You'd be a natural."

Prairie let him stew awhile. She never imagined herself investigating murder like a character out of one of Agatha Christie's books, but she was doing just that. Now that she was in the thick of it, she had an inkling that the only way to get out was to solve it in her own way.

"I don't think I'd fancy that line of work for myself."

"That's too bad." He turned the wheel, rolling into the *Moonlight Diner* parking lot. The bright neon lights flashing against the pink clouded sky. Pulling up to the door, Greenway eased on the brakes to stop the car.

Prairie waited for a minute before forcing a smile. "Thank you for the ride, Detective."

"It was my pleasure."

She opened the door, but just as she was swinging her legs out of the car, Greenway leaned back in his seat and said, "You can't protect him." She paused. "You must know that by now."

Straightening herself, Prairie turned to her left, keeping the glove box in her sights.

"Maybe not." Her eyes shifted to him. "But that doesn't mean I won't try."

"We'll see." He grinned again, friendly like, tipping his hat to her. "You have a nice night now."

She got out of the car and stood in front of the diner until she heard the tires turn and exit the parking lot. The lump in her throat dropped into her stomach, hard and heavy.

It was a relief to be out of that car, but it left her with something new. Something scarier than seeing a wolf man tearing another man apart. She couldn't have known how deep of a line this was, but now she was walking it willingly. And the more she traveled down its winding roads and steep hills, the more dangerous it became.

Chapter 20
The Trash

The night dragged on in a haze. Not even Elliot and Bev's bickering could shake her from how anxious she was. 5 A.M. crept along the face of the clock. Only two more hours before quitting time. It certainly couldn't come soon enough.

"What's gotten into you, Prairie?" Bev asked, leaning against the counter. "You haven't been yourself all morning."

Prairie pressed her lips as she finished sorting the silverware underneath. "Nothing's gotten into me."

"Did Billy misbehave on your date? I swear I'll smack some sense into that boy if you tell me he did."

"It was fine." Prairie paused with a long sigh. "Maybe it wasn't fine." She turned to Bev's concerned stare.

Before she could breathe another word, the front door chimed. Prairie rose to her feet and watched Bernard Hemsworth waltz into the diner. His gray trench coat buttoned to his necktie. A newspaper tucked neatly under his arm. He took off his hat as he stepped up to the counter.

"Mornin' Mr. Hemsworth." Beverly greeted him with a smile. "Fancy a booth or will you be dining at the counter this morning?"

"A booth is fine." His dark down-turned eyes came to Prairie.

"I'll have a number two, over easy with bacon and some coffee. Two creams, no sugar."

Prairie slowly pulled her pad out of her apron, glancing at Beverly who she expected would take him, but he seemed to have her in mind for this morning's unexpected visit.

"All right." Prairie jotted down his order. "I'll get that in for you."

He nodded with a weak smile. "I'll seat myself. Thank you." He walked to the small grouping of booths to the left of the diner, choosing the one facing the far window.

Beverly leaned toward her, keeping her voice low, "Why do you suppose he's here?"

Prairie shrugged. "Beats me. He knows my daddy's not here till seven."

"Maybe he's not here for your daddy." Prairie met Bev's gaze, her eyes flashing with concern. "Want me to take the order when it's ready?"

Prairie's stomach started to turn and twist into small unmanageable knots. She didn't know if Billy would tell his uncle about his personal life, but this visit seemed less like a coincidence the more she thought about it.

"No, it's okay." Prairie breathed as she ripped the ticket from her pad, "I'll take care of it." She pinned the order in the window and poured his coffee. She walked to the booth where Bernard sat and placed it in front of him. "Here you are."

Bernard was reading the paper, keeping it turned toward the window so he could reach with his left hand to slip his fingers through the handle of the mug. "Thank you."

Prairie lingered, but he didn't look up at her or attempt to engage in any sort of conversation. "Your food will be out in just a minute."

He nodded after slurping a hefty helping of coffee into his mouth and continued to scan the paper. Prairie stepped back to return to her duties behind the counter, but him being there kept her on edge. Like Miss. Marple when she had a sinking suspicion but just couldn't peg it.

"Order up!" Elliot rang the bell and slid Mr. Hemsworth's meal into the window. Prairie hurried over and grabbed it from the shelf, taking a few extra napkins. The bacon had that smoky salted smell that she usually loved to indulge in, but now left her head aching and stomach uneasy.

"Number two, all ready for you." She said as she slid the plate onto his table.

Bernard put the paper down and looked down at the plate. "Looks good, as always." He glanced up at her, his expression calm. "Bet you're wondering what I'm doing here."

Prairie placed a set of utensils down. "The thought crossed my mind, yes."

"I had a late night and just left the office." He unraveled his fork and knife, and placed it on his plate with a clink. "I didn't have time to eat, so I fancied myself some Moonlight Diner grub."

"That's just fine." Prairie forced a smile as she moved to leave. "Enjoy your meal."

"You and William." Bernard said as he began cutting through his eggs, the yolk spilling open like the throat of the man from the other night. "How are you two getting along?"

Prairie swallowed. Her mouth running dry. "Oh." Her hands came together in front of her. "We're just fine."

He hummed, nodding slightly as he dipped his toast into the gooey yellow of the yolk. "William is taken with you. Has been for some time." He took a bite of his soaked toast, chewing carefully before placing it back on his plate. "I'm beginning to think he'd do just about anything to make you his girl." He eyed her curiously as his tongue passed between his teeth and upper lip.

"I . . ." Prairie's hands felt slick as she pressed them against her apron. "I suppose he might."

Bernard flashed a quick smile. "I have no qualms with you. I think you're a lovely girl. Maybe a bit too headstrong but lovely nonetheless." He slid his hand through the handle of his coffee mug.

"But I think it's best if you . . . keep William at a distance."

Prairie shifted in her stance. "I'm . . . not sure what you mean."

Bernard turned in the booth to face her more. "You're a distraction, and if William wants to be a partner in what me and his father have built, he needs to stay the course. Keep on a straight path. Not be . . . fraternizing with girls with ambition." He brought the mug to his lips, slurping down another mouthful before carefully drawing it away. "Do you understand, Miss. O'Shea?"

Prairie's toes curled in her shoes. She wasn't sure what to say or do. Her head was all sorts of mixed up, not knowing which way was up or down. Despite his casual tone, she couldn't help but feel like this was a warning. "Are you threatening me, Mr. Hemsworth?"

Bernard chuckled to himself, shaking his head. "Threatening you? Come now, Miss. O'Shea. This is merely me asking a favor. For William's benefit." He placed the mug back on the table. "Surely you want what is best for him, don't you? You've been friends for so long."

"Of course." Was all she had left to say. She was too tired. Too hurt and confused all at the same time.

"Well, we seem to have found ourselves on level ground then." He lifted his fork. "Now, I'd like to continue my meal." He turned back to the table, glancing at her. "I appreciate your cooperation, Miss. O'Shea."

Prairie gave a curt nod before scurrying back toward the doors of the diner. Beverly was standing at one of the booths, refilling the salt and pepper shakers. When she saw Prairie approach, she dropped what she was doing and stepped away.

"Prairie." She uttered. "You look awful." She glanced back at Bernard's booth. "Did he say something?"

Prairie closed her eyes, not sure what to think of Bernard Hemsworth's attempts to keep her away from his nephew. "He . . . wants me to keep away from Billy."

"What? Why on earth—"

"I don't know." Prairie looked at her friend with tired eyes. "And I don't care to know."

"Prairie." Beverly placed a hand on her with a sigh. "What happened with you and Billy on your date? It's got you all shaken up. And now Mr. Hemsworth coming here." She rubbed up and down Prairie's arm to stir up some mild comfort.

"We got in a fight."

"I knew it." Beverly shook her head. "That jerk throwing his weight around. Who does he think he is?" She pulled Prairie into a hug. "You poor thing, having to deal with that no good wheelhouse."

Prairie held on to her friend, laying across her shoulder and closing her eyes. She didn't know how much she needed to feel this. How she was before knowing what she knew, like she was still put together. Even if Beverly wasn't partial to everything.

"You need a ride home later?" Beverly asked softly.

Prairie nodded, pulling away from her but keeping their arms locked. A pair of tears trickled down her face. Beverly wiped them clear off, kissing her forehead before offering another hug. "I got you, sweetie. He's gonna answer to me next time."

"Sorry to break this up." Elliot's voice came from the service window. "But could one of you take out the trash?"

Bev grunted and spun around. "You're cruisin', Elliot! Leave us alone."

"No, it's okay." Prairie sniffed. "I gotta keep busy to keep my mind off things."

"Don't you worry 'bout Mr. Hemsworth." Beverly assured her. "I'll take care of his table."

She left Beverly's side and headed through the kitchen. Elliot gave her a weak smile as she gathered up the full trash barrels and headed out the back toward the dumpsters.

"Sorry to see you so low, Prairie." Elliot's genuine concern stopped her at the door. "But you're tough as nails, you are."

Glancing at Elliot, she gave him a smile. "Thanks for saying so."

He nodded and returned to his duties. Prairie went through the doors, dragged the canisters across the back lot. The sun was creeping over the trees, painting the clouds a deep purple. A faint wind trickled through, drying the dampness that still lingered on her cheeks.

Prairie stopped at the dumpster to tie off the bags. There was too much weighing on her mind to think clearly even with the fresh morning air seeping into her lungs. As she moved to toss it into the rusty iron box, somebody came out from behind it. She jumped clear out of her skin, dropping the bag to clutch at her chest.

"Marrok, for God's sake!" She breathed as her eyes caught his polished leather jacket and gray tee. "You scared me half to death."

Marrok held up his hands. "I didn't mean to scare ya."

It took a few more heavy breaths to recover from the initial jolt. After she settled, it beat from exhilaration weaved with unwanted fear. "What are you doing here? Taking out the trash again?"

Marrok folded his lips, his tongue licking the top as he glanced back at the diner to make sure no one else was around. "I need to talk to ya."

She sighed, wanting the answers but not wanting to risk the unwanted attention. "Fine. But not here. I gotta work still." She took a step toward him, stopping herself before she let the longing get the better of her.

"Wait at the picnic area right outside Oak Springs. I'll meet you there."

Tension pulled between them. Marrok moved in, and the deep forest scent of him knocked her off balance. She reached out her hand, stopping him as his chest met her palm. "What are you waiting for?"

His fingers laced around her wrist, catching her gaze. Prairie wanted to swim in the pools of his eyes, have him capture her in his arms, and tell her he'd never let her go. But this new fear that siphoned through her veins when she looked at him couldn't be overlooked. Her fingers coiled his shirt to her palm. She closed her mouth, holding back the desire she wanted so badly to feed.

"Get out of here. Please." Her voice was but a whisper, but Marrok consented, letting go of her wrist and falling away from her.

Prairie quickly threw the trash into the dumpster and beelined back toward the diner.

Their shift was finally over and both Beverly and Prairie walked out to Bev's car. Beverly flipped her dark brown hair across her right shoulder, pulling her keys from her bag. The light was above the trees now, welcoming another sun filled morning.

Prairie waited for her to find her keys at the front of the car, pulling her sweater over her name tag. She scanned the parking lot, noticing a beat-up brown Ford and a familiar face walking toward her.

"Hold on, Bev." Prairie raised her hand. "I gotta talk to someone."

Bev looked up as Prairie walked to meet Fiona. She had on a checkered red and white dress, her hair tied up in a tail swishing behind her head. Prairie didn't wait to give her a hug, which Fiona took gladly.

"You're looking better." Prairie sighed with relief as they pulled apart. "Doing okay?"

"Yes, thanks to you." Fiona smiled, her eyes drawing with concern. "You doing all right?"

Prairie shrugged, letting go of an unsettled breath. "I don't really know."

Fiona didn't press, maybe seeing there was nothing for it. Prairie wouldn't tell her what she saw in the woods even if she begged. It was better left alone, and Fiona seemed accepting of that.

"I wanted to come and thank you again. My daddy is . . . he's singing your praises to everyone."

"Hello, there." Bev came up behind them with a smile.

Prairie turned to meet her. "Beverly, this is Fiona."

"Pleasure to make your acquaintance, Fiona." Beverly leaned forward to Fiona's shy curtsy. "That dress looks keen on you."

"Thank you very much." Fiona looked back to Prairie. "I'm sorry. I . . . put you in that position—"

"It wasn't your doing." Prairie took her hand. "You didn't do anything wrong."

A car door shut and caught all their attention. Billy shoved his hands in his pants pockets as he made his way to the diner, not realizing Prairie was standing in the parking lot.

"That rat showing his face here after what he'd done to you?" Beverly sneered. "I'll give him a talking to."

Prairie reached for her friend, "Bev. You don't have to."

"He's gotta understand just because you got green doesn't mean you gotta treat people like dirt." She flashed a smile. "If you'll excuse me."

She hurried toward them, stopping with her arms folded and hip popped right in front of Billy. Prairie couldn't hear what she was saying, but Billy's face dropped as her words hit. He glanced back at Prairie as Beverly continued her assault.

"He won't know what hit him after Bev is done with him."

Fiona whipped her head back around the second Billy looked over, her eyes shifting and chest practically heaving.

Prairie squinted, "What's wrong?"

Fiona looked at her, her head shaking as her mouth fell open to silence. Prairie lowered her voice as she placed a supporting hand on Fiona's shoulder.

"Fiona . . ."

"That's him." Fiona whispered. "That's my date."

Prairie looked back up to where Billy was. "That's . . . that can't be." She came back to her. "You must not be seeing straight."

"No. It's him." Fiona's eyes grew. "It's Desmond. My white knight."

"Desmond?" Prairie's wheels started turning. "That's not Desmond. Desmond was his . . . daddy's name." Prairie flashed from Billy back to Fiona again, taking her arms. "He called you at the club?"

"Yes." Fiona nodded. "He came and got me. I'd only met him a few days before."

"In Oak Springs . . ." Prairie's gaze hit the parking lot. "You met him in Oak Springs." That day at the dress shop. It all made sense now. He was there. And Fiona. She was the girl. The girl he was flirting with. The girl he called after Prairie ended their date on the street.

"Prairie." Fiona grasped her tightly. "Who is he?"

Prairie sucked air into her lungs and narrowed her eyes. "Fiona. Don't stay here, okay?"

"Who is he?"

"If he calls you again, don't talk to him."

"But *who is he,* Prairie?"

Beverly came waltzing back looking pleased as punch. "I think I talked some sense into that good for nothing. You won't have any more trouble from Billy Hemsworth as long as he knows what's good for him." She looked from Prairie to Fiona. "Everything okay?"

"Yes. We're fine." Prairie forced a smile, her eyes falling on Billy who was looking at her good. When Fiona turned, he hurriedly climbed back into his Bel-Air, slamming the door before backing up to exit the lot.

"We gotta get going." Prairie looked at Fiona. "Get home safe, you hear?"

Fiona nodded excessively, looking at Beverly. "It was nice to meet you, ma'am." She turned on her heels and walked to her car, getting in fast.

"She gonna be all right?" Bev asked as Fiona pulled out of the parking lot.

"I hope so." Prairie turned to her friend, pressing her teeth together. "I need you to take me somewhere."

Chapter 21
The Answers

"Why am I taking you to the picnic spot, Prairie?" Bev narrowed her eyes as they continued down the highway. "I'm not leaving you there, am I?"

"I'm . . . meeting someone." Prairie waited as she pulled at the buttons of her sweater. "You don't need to stay."

"Who you meeting there?" They waited in silence as Prairie hoped to tell her as little as possible. "I'm not taking you if you don't tell me who."

"You'll see when we get there." Bev shot her a daggered look. Prairie could feel the tense frustration oozing from her eyes. She hated keeping the truth from her friend, but the less Beverly knew, the better.

The rest of the car ride was silent. Prairie held her breath as they approached the picnic area sign, but Beverly pulled off the exit, and rolled the car over the dirt path to the open lot dotted with trees and wooden picnic tables. The only car there was Marrok's dark Thunderbird.

As Beverly rolled into a spot and cut the engine, she stared at the black chariot with a stern look. "Whose car is that?"

Prairie didn't wait and swung open the door, letting herself out. Beverly followed suit, catching her just before she could es-

cape from her question. The moment Prairie came around the back, Marrok slid out. A smoke lodged between his lips as he came up the side, leaning against the cab like the cool, slick greaser he was.

"The drifter." Beverly grabbed Prairie's arm and swung her round. "This doesn't feel right, Prairie. What's going on with you?"

"I can't tell you." Prairie begged as her words caught in her throat. "Not yet."

"I am not leaving you here with that man." Bev glanced at him. "I don't like this one bit."

"You gotta trust me. He won't do anything. I swear to you, he won't. But you can't stay. Please." Beverly found her desperate eyes, settling on them with quiet concern. "Please, Beverly."

Beverly looked from Marrok and back to Prairie, fighting back the urge to run him off with her mouth. But after a solid deep breath, she stood up on her toes and bellowed to him. "One hair on her head out of place and you'll answer to me! You got that?"

Marrok gave a single nod, waiting patiently as Bev clutched Prairie around the neck. "You call me as soon as you can, or I'll come back with Georgie. You hear me?"

"I will. I'll call you." Prairie tightened her grasp on Bev before pulling away. "Don't tell anybody, okay?"

"All right." Bev went to the car and opened the door. "Call me." Prairie stepped away as the car purred to life. Beverly gave her one more straight look as she pulled out of the parking lot and back on to the highway.

A slow turn brought Marrok back into focus. Prairie lowered her chin, taking each step with careful consideration. She wasn't sure she was ready to hear what he had to say, but damn if she didn't need to hear it.

She stopped a few feet from him, the smoke still resting comfortably in his mouth. Marrok only watched her, hands deep in his jean pockets. He didn't look anything but how he always did. If it weren't for his eyes, shifting this way and that like he couldn't see straight, Prairie would think he thought nothing of this entire thing.

"You wanted to talk," Prairie breathed, "so talk."

Marrok threw his smoke to the ground, not bothering to snuff it out. "I apologize." He finally locked eyes with her. "I never meant for you to get mixed up in all this."

"But I did, and now, here I am."

Marrok breathed. "Here you are."

She folded her arms, trying to keep herself from breaking apart more than she already was.

"So, what are you? A wolf man?"

Marrok brought his hand to his chin, cradling it before dragging his fingers down to the point. "Not exactly."

"Well, then *what* exactly?"

He reached behind his head, and rubbed the back of his neck as if trying to find the words. "All right." His hand fell to his side. "I am. Whatcha said. A wolf man, but not like in the movies. Not like that."

Prairie's words shortened her breath. "Then like what?"

"I don't need a full moon to turn, but I can only turn at night. A full moon just makes it easier. I got control over what I do. I'm never not myself, and I can heal quick. It's pretty hard to hurt me, but I ain't unkillable."

Prairie heard what he said but still couldn't wrap a finger around it. It all seemed untrue, but that was fool's talk in her mind. She knew it was true. All of it. "How?" She muttered, "How'd this happen to you?"

Marrok sighed, taking a step away from the car. "I told you about my family. 'Bout what happened. I was dead with a bullet in my head. The man who found me . . . it was the only way he could save me."

"So, he . . . changed you? Infected you?"

"Call it what you want."

Prairie shook her head. "This is crazy." She broke into a short stride, pacing back and forth with her hands hanging in front of her, trying to grasp onto his words. "This can't be real." She shook out her hands.

"I don't expect you to understand."

Her feet crunched in the dirt as she turned to him. "You're a murderer!"

Marrok's tongue pushed his bottom lip out as her accusation sunk in. "That's all I got, Prairie. It's all I can do to not be what they make a monster out to be. It's how I can do right."

"Takin' out the trash?" Prairie squinted. "Is that what you're calling killing people?"

Marrok sucked in deep through his nostrils. "The man who found me, he was the same. He showed me how to use this for good. To make a difference in this backwards world we live in."

"Is that why you're here?"

He gave a single nod. "Colored girls are being taken and never seen again from all over these parts. So, I was called in to find out who's takin' them."

"Who called you? The police?" Her tone softened, listening to the truth of his words.

"I don't work for no badge. It's people who find me and tell me their troubles and pray to God I'm the answer. I don't claim to be no God, there's only one of them, but I'll take what I got and use it to help them."

She shook her head, "There's got to be another way other than killing people, Marrok."

The sharpness in his eyes sent a bolt of fear down her spine. He looked how he did when he first walked into the diner that rainy morning. Like he was sizing her up, waiting for her to do something to give him an excuse to act. It was the wolf in him. She understood that far too well now.

"There ain't no other way," his tone hardened. "This is how it's gotta be, and I'd rather do something with it than be like those bastards that slaughtered my family like pigs," he pointed out toward the road, "Them's the real monsters. Killin' without a cause. Blinded by their own reflections of what a man should and shouldn't be."

Anger wafted from him like a heat wave. All the hairs on her arms stood straight up, cooking the blood beneath her skin. He was right. Every word of it. What they did was unforgivable. No words or laws could make it right. She didn't know if they were ever caught or what might have happened after they shot Marrok. But Prairie could only imagine it wasn't anything good.

"You're right, Marrok," she said, keeping her words calm, "of course you're right."

Marrok combed his fingers through his hair, stepping left then right. His jaw was tight, like he was trying to hold something back he didn't want getting out.

"People like me," he turned to her, pulling at his jacket, "get put down from the moment we're born until the day we die." He came closer, casting a shadow across Prairie's face. "If I can make their lives just a little easier by stoppin' them who want to make it hard, then I will. Because we're all people, Prairie. Born with the same parts in the same way. I know you see it that way too."

He drew back, keeping his eyes on hers. Prairie's ribs could barely cage her frantic heart, thumping so hard it ached. That smoky aroma of him brought her back to last night, standing together under the moon.

All the times he showed up out of the blue. Every single one, Prairie had a feeling now more than ever, it wasn't just a coincidence. He had a reason for being there. For running into her and talking to her. Maybe part of it was curiosity, but that couldn't be all it was. Knowing what he was doing here, he wasn't drifting.

He was hunting.

"Why did you come to the Moonlight that morning?"

Marrok sniffed, rolling his tongue along his bottom lip and looked away. "I was followin' somethin'."

"What were you following?"

He looked at her again, "a scent."

She closed her eyes, taking a deep breath, "You stopped on the road that day. Not because it was right—"

"It was right. I never lied about that."

"But it was something else," she opened them again, staring deep into his smooth brown eyes, "right?"

He braced his hand at his sides, "I didn't know then, when I stopped to help ya. I didn't know if it was you or—"

"Billy." Prairie hung her head. "It was Billy." Her eyes shut, not wanting to believe herself.

If Billy was taking them girls . . .

"Fiona said Billy was the one who called her that night at the club."

"Whatcha mean?"

She looked up at him, her lips pressing together. "I saw them together. I thought I was seeing things, but now . . . Fiona said she was meeting someone that night. It was Billy. He lied about his name. He was with her when she was . . . when she was . . ." She clenched her eyes tight, trying to convince herself to stop, but nothing could stop this, even if she wished it with all her heart. Why Billy's been acting so shifty. So unhinged. This all made sense now. More than she wanted it to.

"She was at the diner this morning. Billy came by and scared her half to death. He didn't say anything. But Fiona, there wasn't a doubt in her mind about who he was."

Prairie's stomach turned as she tried to swallow the sick down. "You think Billy's been taking those girls?"

The corner of his lips turned. "No, but I think he's the bait used to reel them in."

The hook sank deep. Prairie closed her eyes, knowing what she had to do. If she ever wanted this mystery to be solved, she couldn't stand around and wait. She was here now. All the secrets were out in the open, ready for her to act. "You need him."

She opened her eyes to Marrok's stoic silence, watching her with careful eyes, unable to let his answer fall from his closed lips. Prairie waited as her heart rattled her ribcage.

"*Damn it*, Marrok." She closed the gap between them with a few heavy strides. "Do you need him?"

Marrok searched the fine lines of her profile, seemingly connecting the freckles adorning her face like a star-crossed sky before giving a single nod. The perfume of him hit her like a brick wall, but she had to keep it together. Tightening her fists at her sides, she forced hot air from her nostrils.

"Fine. I'll get him for you." She took a step back as he grabbed her arm.

"No."

"You said it yourself." She yanked away from him. "I wasn't meant to be dragged into this. But I'm here now. I'm in it. Might as well be useful."

Marrok tilted his head. "Prairie—"

"*Don't . . .*" she lifted her hand in front of her, turning her head slightly to avoid his pleading gaze. ". . . don't talk me out of it. I'm doing it and that's that." Her fingers folded in her palm, all except her pointer as she directed it at him.

"You don't hurt him, you hear me? Billy is a lot of things. But he ain't bad. He's . . . just trying to find his way."

His chest rose with an intake of air. "You have my word. But if he hurts you—"

"He won't." She moved to the car and opened the passenger side door. "Now, take me home. I gotta make a phone call."

Chapter 22
The Call

"Hello?" Prairie loosened her fist at her chest as she clung to the receiver. "Billy, I'm glad I caught you."

"Prairie." Billy shifted on the other line. "I thought you were done with me."

"I wanted to call you and . . . apologize. For Bev and . . . how I acted the other night."

He breathed into the receiver, muffling the sound. "I understand why Bev said what she said, and I wish I didn't leave you like that. I'm sorry too. I wasn't thinking straight."

"I don't blame you for anything."

"Where did you go after?"

"Just home." There was a long silence. Prairie glanced at Marrok who stood against the wall facing her, watching as the conversation started to stray from the course.

"Well, thank you for calling me." Billy sighed. "I gotta get going."

Prairie raised on her tiptoes. "Are you free later?"

"Free?"

Prairie licked her lips and turned slightly away from Marrok. "To take me to work?"

"You just looking for a ride or do you actually wanna see me?"

Prairie twisted the cord between her fingers. "Can't it be both?"

Silence crept along the line. Prairie bit her lip as she waited for him to answer her, but all she could hear was his breathing, "Billy?"

"Who were you talking to this morning at the diner?"

"What . . . oh," Prairie leaned against the wall, twisting the phone chord through her fingers, "Some girl asking for directions is all."

"You sure that's all?"

Prairie glanced at Marrok, "Why are you so hung up about someone asking for directions?"

Billy went silent again, but he didn't drag it out as long this time, maybe worried she would start asking too many questions if he didn't button it quick, "I'm not. I just . . . want to make sure you're not trying to jive me or anything."

"When's the last time I did something like that?" she didn't want to wait for him to answer, "So, you will, right? You'll pick me up?"

"Okay," he finally said, "I'll pick you up at eight."

"Make it seven thirty. We can . . . talk. Just drive a bit."

Another silence left her hanging on her last breath. Prairie waited, still hearing him on the other end. "Since when do you like to *just drive*?"

"Since today."

For him to think she would say such a thing wasn't entirely out of the blue. Prairie was always forward, so why would her wanting this sound any different? But there was still a tight string being pulled as she waited for his answer. Part of her knew he couldn't resist the chance, but maybe, after the other night, it was enough for him to say no.

"Alright, seven thirty. You best get some sleep then."

Prairie let herself breathe again. "I'll see you later, then."

"Bye now."

She hung up the phone, collecting herself before turning to Marrok. "He's coming. I'll ask him to stop at the picnic area on the highway. You better be on time."

Her hand finally came off the receiver, trying to come to terms with what was about to happen. She couldn't believe she was doing this. Was it for Marrok? For Billy? For those innocent girls going missing? She didn't really know. There was a small part of her that felt she was doing it for herself. Though she couldn't believe how fast everything had turned, like the pages of one of Christie's crime stories.

"What's this guy to you anyways?" Marrok's question was laced with a hint of jealousy, or maybe it was malice now that he was certain what Billy was up to.

Prairie wanted to snap back at him, saying it wasn't any of his business. But sense told her it might help him understand why she just couldn't let Billy go, despite him treating her like he had. Everything Marrok saw of him was negative. This was her chance to prove, in her own way, that Billy wasn't a lost cause.

"We're childhood friends." She began, keeping her gaze steady on him. "Our families were very close, and when we got to high school, I was his girl. For a while."

Marrok stayed silent, listening while wrestling back his distaste for the subject. "After we graduated, I said I didn't want to be with him anymore. Then his folks died in a terrible car wreck. I couldn't let him be alone, but I couldn't give him what he wanted either." Her gaze fell to her fingers lacing into the phone cord.

"He never stopped asking me, again and again, to be his girl. Sometimes I see the old Billy in him, how he was before everything happened. A part of me holds onto that, wishing he'd stop being how he is. Even if he did change though, if I did say yes, it would never work."

"Why is that?" Marrok's question shifted her gaze to him.

"I want too much. That's what got me into this mess in the first place. The wanting." She scoffed, dropping the cord with a shrug. "I guess I got what I asked for."

Ambition wasn't what most found to be an admirable quality, but she wasn't raised to be anything else. She couldn't be close-minded and not want for herself. Marrok was the only one who saw what kind of girl she really was. That was what captivated her about him. The mystery and the confidence he carried, even the attitude, kept her there.

"I should hate you."

The corner of Marrok's mouth twitched. "You got every right to."

She lurched forward a tad. "You used me."

Marrok looked down at the checkered floor. "At first, and I should have stopped. I should have left you alone once I got the trail straight. I didn't want you to get hurt."

"Hurt like those girls, you mean?"

He shook his head, bringing himself back up to face her. His mouth opened, but no words came out before closing again like a bear trap. Every muscle in her body was on edge. Her lungs tightened in her chest as her hands pressed into her stomach. Whatever he was going to say, she knew it was going to pack a punch she might not get up from.

The minute dragged out in deafening silence before Marrok took a deep breath, letting his words out with an exhale, "I was scared of you, Prairie."

The air caught in her throat as he continued to speak. "Scared of what you did to me. The day you sat in my car, and I took ya to the diner. After you went inside and I was all alone, you lingered. You gave me something I never thought I'd ever have again. Something I don't deserve to have."

He slid across the wall to get closer to her. Prairie rocked on her heels, her back falling against the wall. Nothing could distract her from him. Her heart fluttered with the butterflies let loose in her stomach.

"What did I give you?"

Marrok carefully took her hand, letting her palm fall open as he rested it in his. He traced lines across her skin, sending shivers down her spine that quickened her pulse. "Wheat. Blowin' in a summer breeze. Quiet nights sparkling with fireflies in the moonlight. My mama's coffee, wafting on the fire, the first bitter taste she enjoyed before the sun came up."

His fingers grasped her own, drawing her in. "There's nothing left of who I was, back before all this. But you took me home, Prairie. Nobody ever has an' I don't think nobody ever will."

Red flushed her speckled cheeks as his words melted any ill taste that remained from his secret. "You sure know how to make a girl feel special."

"I ain't saying it to make you feel special." His fingers lingered up her arm, to the curve of her collar bone before coming to cradle her neck. "I'm saying it because it's the truth. I knew what my path was after I became what I am, an' finding home was never supposed to be part of that." His thumb brushed under her ear, sending goose pimples all over her skin.

"I can't be selfish," the dull scent of coffee and turned earth flooded her lungs, "but I want to be."

She reached out to cling on the edge of his leather jacket, pulling him into a tempting position. "It won't be easy, Marrok."

"It's a chance. A chance you either take or you don't." He brushed his stout nose against her own.

"An' I want to take it . . . but . . . I don't know if I can." They stayed there, hovering just out of reach. Neither of them brave enough to take that chance and damn everyone else to hell for saying it was wrong.

"I'll go," he said in a hushed tone, "just say the word and you'll never see me again."

"I don't want you to go." pulling him closer, his chest came to rest against her. She couldn't hear anything but the sound of her heart and felt nothing but the rapid pounding of his. She was tired of waiting for the life she wanted, tired of waiting for others to be okay so she could finally take that first step. This was it. The call she needed to answer for her to break free from everything that was holding her back: from her folks, from Billy, even from the wrongs that the world deemed right.

"I don't want to wait anymore."

He smiled, bringing his succulent lips a breath from hers. "That makes two of us."

She was ready to fall. To taste him and feel him close to her now and every minute that came after. They brushed against each other, drawing out the thirst she couldn't help but quench. Marrok tilted her head, turning into the angle of her face to give her what her entire body was pining for.

The phone rang, jumping Prairie out of her skin. Marrok's head shot back a bit, a sly smile gracing his scarred face. "You better get that."

They lingered in a few drawn out breaths, each tempting the other just by being there. Marrok's hand finally left her, allowing her to reach up toward the phone to answer.

"Hello. O'Shea residence."

"*Prairie!*" Beverly practically screamed. "You never called me!"

"I'm sorry, Beverly. I . . . I got held up." She turned to face the wall. Marrok came up behind her, moving the loose waves of her hair, exposing her neck. Prairie shuttered at his touch on her pale Irish skin.

"What happened with that drifter you're keepin' all bottled up to yourself. He didn't hurt you, did he?"

"No . . . he didn't. I . . . just needed to talk to him, is all." Marrok pressed his nose to her skin, the heat from his lungs tracing a line down her collar bone toward the back of her ear.

"You sure you're all right? You need me to come get you for work later?"

Prairie could barely hold the phone in her hand, tilting to the right as if to clear the way for his touch. "No. Thank you though. I . . . I'll see you later."

"You sure?"

"Yeah, I'm just tired. It's been . . . a long day."

"Prairie." Bev's voice faded as Marrok moved to her jawline, pressing his forehead to her temple, his soft lips on her cheeks. "You better tell me what's going on."

"Okay . . ." her voice shuttered from the yearning that was stirring up inside her, making her weak in the knees. "I will. At work . . . cross my heart."

"If you don't show up, I swear I'll call the police."

"Goodbye, Bev." She shut the phone on the receiver and turned, back pressed to the wall.

Marrok wavered in his stance, looking at her. The corner of his mouth coming up into a wide grin. Her hand moved to her neck where the footprints of his breath still lingered. Her chest heaved with anticipation, the wanting never leaving her skin as he backed away. She followed him from the hall to the front door. He pulled it open from behind, stepping into the threshold.

"I should go," he held up his palm to her. Prairie gently slid hers along the fine lines and cool smoothness of his ringed fingers. He grasped it, bringing her hand to his lips and placing a kiss on her skin. It radiated an unimaginable warmth that ran down her arm and across her chest, trailing down her torso to the tips of her toes.

"Sleep well now, Miss. Prairie."

She smiled, letting him slip through the door and down the

walkway. Prairie watched him get into his dark chariot. The engine roared to life with the slow crunch along the drive as he backed into the street. His eyes caught hers for a moment. She wanted to run down to him, but better judgment told her otherwise. All she could do was keep that smile for him, which he returned with a charm-filled grin before peeling from the house and breaking out onto the road.

Chapter 23
The Plan

"So, what is this all about?" Billy asked with a smugness that Prairie almost didn't recognize. As confident as she was, she didn't know what Marrok planned to do to get the truth out of Billy. The only thing that allowed her to breathe easy was his promise he wouldn't hurt him. What that meant to a wolf man, remained to be seen.

"What do you mean?"

"Don't jive me, Prairie. This is about something." He glanced at her as the car continued down the road. "Where'd you go after I left you the other night?"

"Nowhere. I took the bus home, that's all."

"That Jack didn't take you, did he?"

"I didn't ask him."

Billy shook his head, keeping his hand locked on the wheel, "You're not one to lie, Prairie, but I think you are."

Prairie took a breath, daring herself to make a move to prove to Billy nothing was amiss. If she wasn't able to convince him to stop at the picnic area, all this would be for nothing.

"I was cross with you! After pulling all that on my birthday, of all days! I was a wreck after you left. And your uncle breathing down my neck about it—"

"Hold it, hold it." Billy glanced at her, the tightness in his jaw melting as his eyes came into focus, "He talked to you?"

Prairie bit her lip, clutching her hands together in the lap of her skirt, "He told me to stay away from you, Billy. Like I was causing something bad being around you."

A cautious glance caught Billy dragging his hand down his chin. There was something boiling under his skin now at the mention of Bernard's involvement. His mouth clenched, a sharp exhale scraping the sides of his nostrils as he breathed.

"You're not his business. He had no right to say anything to you."

She put a hand on his arm. Billy eyed their connection, raising a smooth brow. Glancing over at her, Prairie leaned against him, trying to play any card she could pull to keep him from remembering his suspicions of her.

"I'm not a thorn in your side, am I, Billy?"

The tension in his muscles eased to her closeness. "Never. You . . . you're all I got, Prairie."

Hearing him say those words twisted her gut. She knew how isolated he had been since his folks died. And being under Bernard's eye was enough pressure to blow a gasket. Part of her knew what she meant to Billy, but to hear it made it more real. It made what she was planning to do that much more painful.

"I'm sorry, Billy. I didn't mean to make things hard on you." Her hand moved up to trace the hairs at the base of his hairline. "Maybe I was wrong about keeping you at arm's length."

He cocked a brow, "You sweet talking me?"

She leaned back, tilting her head on the seat to look dreamily at him. "I ain't as easy as Bev, you can't expect me to be."

"That's what I like about you, Prairie." He had a keen sparkle in his sky-blue eyes and that charming confidence painted clean across his face. "You make me work for it."

It was too easy to lure him in, especially after mentioning

Bernard's attempt to stop anything between them. She knew Billy was keen to please his uncle, but when it came to her, there wasn't anyone who could tell him no, and she'd seen him fight like hell to prove it.

She glanced at the window, the picnic area coming up on their left. "Why don't we . . . park a while then?"

Nerves rattled her ribcage as he pulled into the picnic area. She wasn't sure if she could keep this up, but she had to try. The car stopped at the farthest spot where the trees cast the most shadow. Marrok's car was nowhere in sight. They were the only ones there.

Prairie laid back in her seat, trying to control her breathing. With a slow turn, Billy killed the engine. He placed his arm on the back of her headrest and looked at her. "So, we've parked. What now?"

She hesitated, unsure what would come next. It's not like she never parked before with Billy, but this was different. Maybe she could try to remember those days, back when life was less heavy That's how she had to be, if only for a few more minutes. "Maybe you should show me?"

He watched her for a minute, eyes searching her face, "You sure you want this?"

Prairie didn't expect him to be mindful of her wants right now. This was the first time she had even suggested they do anything like this since they broke up. It pinched at her heart, seeing him care like this, genuinely care. It made this whole situation so much harder. Knowing the old Billy was still in there, just begging to come out.

There was no time to sit on it, so Prairie latched onto the collar of his Cuban tee and dragged him down on her. The spicy scent of his ten-dollar cologne overtook her senses. Prairie kept her fingers locked on his shirt so she wouldn't instinctively push him off. Billy crashed his lips on her own, slipping his arm around her to cradle her back. His tongue tried to pry open her mouth, dragging her down a rabbit hole she never thought she'd go down again. She gave in, letting him kiss her like they used to do under the bleachers after his baseball games.

Nostalgia flooded her senses, tickling her skin, and exacerbating the frantic nature of her heart. But it only lasted a few seconds.

Billy's body lurched off her and clean through the car's canvas top. Prairie brought her hand to her mouth in disbelief, watching Marrok toss him from the top of the car.

Billy skirted on his side, but recovered quickly, spitting out a dirt filled wad before sitting up, wiping his arm across his face. "You park ape bastard!"

Prairie scrambled for the lever and practically fell out of the car. She got to her feet as Marrok came down from the hood. He rushed him quick, grabbing him by the shirt and lifting Billy straight off his feet.

Her hand shot out to grab his arm before he could move another inch. "You promised you wouldn't hurt him!"

Marrok's eyes flashed as he cracked his gaze at her. Keeping his mouth thin, his nostrils flared as he dropped Billy like he was tossing a paper in the trash. Billy fell on to his back, propping himself up on his elbows as he regained the air that was knocked from his lungs.

"You . . . you helped this negro?"

Marrok lurched toward him, causing Billy to skid backwards across the ground. "You best only speak when you're spoken to."

Prairie got in front of him. "*Stop.*"

Marrok looked mean, the same toughness she saw when manhandling that jowled gentlemen at the drive-in. But he didn't scare her. If she wanted to keep him under control, she had to stay firm.

"You get outta here. Now," he said, rather gritty.

"You don't tell me when to get. I'm in this just as you are." She tossed her gaze to Billy, not wanting to give in to Marrok's stern brown eyes.

"Where are you taking those girls, Billy?"

Billy chuckled to himself, sitting on the ground with his hands hanging over his knees. "I don't know what you're talking about. You've really gone off your rocker on this one."

"Don't pull the wool over my eyes, Billy." She loomed over him, pointing toward the road. "I saw you with her. Fiona. A few days before our date."

He swallowed, "I have no clue who you're talking about."

Marrok moved to approach him, but Prairie's arm came out to stop him. "No. Let me."

Adjusting her uniform, she knelt down in front of the accused. "Come on, Billy. This ain't you. Luring girls away from their homes. Their loved ones. Who's making you do this?"

Billy rolled his tongue over his bottom teeth, sniffing loudly as he looked away. "Nobody's making me do anything." His face drew red as his hands came up to wrap around the back of his neck. Prairie placed a hand on his knee, watching him long enough that he couldn't avoid her.

"Billy, please." Her voice lowered. "You need to help us stop whoever's doing this."

He watched her, eyes shifting with uncertainty. His chin raised to Marrok who stood stoically in silence. "What's he got to do with all this?"

"He's just trying to help, is all. Their families, the ones already gone. They asked him to find them. But we need your help too, Billy. Please."

They waited quietly. Prairie caught Billy's gaze again, seeing the rumble being fought behind his eyes. With a hard swallow, he folded his lips, biting down hard as if trying to convince himself to keep it shut. "I can't tell you, Prairie. Especially you. You can't be involved. I won't—"

"Billy," she took his face in her hands, keeping him from leaving her sight, "you're better than this. I know who you really are, and it's not this. You say I'm all you got. Well, you'll lose me if you keep this up. I don't want that, but I can't stand by you if you're doing this."

His tongue passed over the lines of his mouth, eyes clamping shut. She could feel his body trembling in her hands, like a child who was hiding from a monster, hoping he'd be invisible. Prairie didn't let go. She waited, holding him so he wouldn't fall to the ground and get lost in whatever demons he was fighting off.

"I just drug 'em, is all." He finally spoke, looking at her again, placing his hands on her wrists, "Then I'm gone. I don't hurt them or know where he's taking them once they leave Oak Springs. I swear."

"Why? Why take them at all?"

"For money, that's why. It's all about money, Prairie. The more you got the more power you have." Billy shrunk back from her hands, looking away as his legs curled up to his chest. "I don't know where they go. I don't want to know. The less I know . . ."

What he was doing, even if he didn't know all of it, was worse than she'd thought. The fact that he was even involved at all made her skin crawl and her heart bleed for him all at once.

"Who is making you do this?"

Prairie searched his fleeting eyes before he settled on her forest greens with a sigh. "Come on, Prairie. I don't need to tell you who."

Prairie settled on the ground as Marrok came behind her, looking down at Billy like he was about to scold a puppy who'd puddled the floor.

"Where?" Marrok boldly asked. "Where you keepin' 'em?"

Billy shot him a glance, "I can show you."

Chapter 24
The Cabin

Prairie sat up front with Billy as he drove cautiously down the road. They were heading out of Oak Springs now, along the outskirts of town where most of the killings had happened. Billy had both hands on the wheel, his fingers tight like he'd been cuffed to the seat. He kept looking from the road to Prairie, like he was hoping this was just her pulling his leg out from under him—a jib, a stitch. But Prairie only watched him, letting her determined stare paint the picture for her.

Marrok sat hunched on the floor behind the driver's seat. Prairie couldn't help but be scared for him, and scared of what Billy might be pulling them into.

The car turned off the road, down a rough and tumble dirt stretch leading deep into the trees. Prairie gazed out the window, searching her memories for an answer as to why this place was so familiar. When the car passed two brick laid pillars flanking the road, chipped and broken from years of abandonment, everything clicked.

"Your cabin." She said, catching Billy's attention.

"You remember?" Billy pressed his lips, "it's been a long time since you've been here."

The Hemsworth cabin was part of her summers when she was a little girl. Billy's parents used to throw lavish summer parties

where they invited the entire town to roast weenies by the fire and sit on the dock, that overlooked their private lake, to watch fireworks crack in the sky.

It had been years since she'd been there and, after Billy's parents died, there was even less of a reason to go back. His uncle claimed to have sold it, kissing any hope of enjoying another perfect summer night there goodbye.

The cabin came creeping up on their right as the road curved. This wasn't a small square hunting cabin. It stood three-stories high with a wrap-around porch that led down to a hidden gem of a lake that the Hemsworth's claimed as their own. There were always lights flickering from the windows in the past, filling the house with life.

Now it was like a ghost, chained by the years of weathering that nature did to all things left to stand alone. All the shutters were closed along its face. Wicker chairs were on their heads, strewn across the porch, colorless and filth ridden.

A heavy sinking feeling crept into Prairie's stomach. Even the trees surrounding the house moved as if beckoning them to flee while they had the chance.

Pulling up to the door, Billy killed the engine. "Here we are." He looked back at Marrok, who quietly rose onto the back seat.

"We don't have much time." Billy unbundled his belt. He kicked the door open and got out of the car. Prairie took a deep breath, quickly following suit. Marrok grabbed her arm before she could leave the safety of the car.

"You stay here."

"Like hell I will." Prairie pulled her arm away steadily, keeping her composure as best she could. "I'm coming with you."

Marrok didn't argue, letting her join Billy at the front of the car. When he met them, he slid between them, his stout nose sucking in the damp forest air. "Get moving."

Billy backed off before turning full tilt, shoving his hands in his slacks as he wrapped around toward the back of the house. Marrok followed behind him, keeping a strong arm in front of Prairie to protect her for whatever they were walking into.

Prairie looked at the sorry state of this once palace in the woods. Some of the windows were cracked, and holes lined the wood along its side, probably inhabited by all sorts of critters. She didn't notice they'd stopped until she walked into Marrok's arm.

Billy stood in front of the cellar door, gray and spotted with rust. He cracked his knuckles, bending down to unlatch the handles. With a short huff, he flung the doors open, letting them moan as the metal fell against the cement surrounding it.

"Down there." He gestured, eyes darting to Marrok briefly. Prairie couldn't say for sure, but Billy was acting scared. Scared of Marrok or something else, she wasn't sure. Nobody else's car was here, so she was certain they were alone.

"You first." Marrok barely moved at his request. With a hard gulp, Billy abided, carefully ascending down the creaky metal steps into the depths below.

Fear brought Prairie's hand to grasp Marrok's arm tight. His dark eyes found hers, pulling her in. "Keep close. I won't let nothing happen to ya."

"I know." She whispered.

The smell of mildew hit her something awful. She brought her hand to her nose to try and keep it from infecting her lungs too severely. Shelves with old gardening tools, dirty gasoline cans, rotten wooden boards and other such things lined the walls. Rope and what looked like animal traps hung from the ceiling, barely an inch from the top of Marrok's head. There wasn't much light aside from what came down from the door, though it was beginning to wane as the sun started to move aside for night to spread over the sky.

Billy stood toward the back of the cellar, next to a tall double-doored wardrobe. "In here."

"There?" Prairie moved past Marrok, taking a stand beside Billy. "You best be telling the truth, Billy."

"I have nothing left to hide." He said sternly but looked at Prairie like he wanted to run as bad as a jack rabbit from a coyote.

He opened the doors, fishing his hand inside and switched on a light. Instead of old jackets and musty suits hanging from the rod, a passageway glowed in front of them with gray concrete walls opening into a large, lifeless room.

Along the far wall were rows and rows of wooden doors with small iron-barred windows at the top. It wasn't until a pair of fingers and frightened eyes peered out from behind one of the doors, that Prairie lurched forward in a frantic run.

"Prairie." Billy called to her, but she didn't listen. She stepped into the room, guided by the hands beckoning her to grasp them.

"My God." The girl's hand was caked in dirt and soot. Her eyes stricken with fear, laid deep into the wells of her dark face.

Billy stepped into the room, looking down at the floor. Two other doors came alive with frightened faces, the girls looking from Billy to Prairie, wondering why she was even there.

"We'll get you out of here." She turned around as Marrok came though. The other girls fluttered in relief filled sighs.

"He's here!" They gasped. "He's here to save us!"

"Come here." Prairie looked back at the girl whose hand she grasped. "What's your name?"

"I'm . . . I'm Clarabelle." She muttered with a shaken voice.

"Clarabelle." Prairie worked hard not to seem scared out of her wits. "My name is Prairie. We're getting you out of here."

"No." Clarabelle pulled her hand into the bars. "You gotta leave. If he finds you here . . ." she glanced at Billy, eyes barely blinking as if knowing something was due to come that nobody was expecting.

"It's okay." Prairie assured her as Marrok got to the door. A heavy padlock kept the door latch in place. Marrok grasped it in his hand. Gritting his teeth, he ripped it free without breaking a sweat. Prairie dropped Clarabelle's hand as Marrok took over their haphazard escape.

She turned and stormed up to Billy like a freight train. Her hand cut across his face, pushing him to the right and forcing his hand to cradle the blow.

"You're despicable, William Hemsworth," she growled. "How could you do something like this?"

Billy swallowed his pride, coming back with her handprint glowing on the surface of his cheek. "I don't have a choice, Prairie."

"No choice?"

He stayed silent, holding his breath to keep the truth from spilling out.

"You best open your mouth, Billy."

"Take her to the car." Marrok came behind her with Clarabelle clutched to his arm in a sullied peach dress and broken shoes. "I'll get him talking."

"No, you will not!" Prairie glared at him. "We're not doing this your way." She watched his cold glare, but there was nothing cold about him to her. "You said you wouldn't hurt a hair on his head. So, take care of the girls and I'll get your answers."

Marrok waited with calm determination before heeding her word and falling back into the passageway.

Billy watched him disappear before turning back to Prairie. "You asked him not to hurt me?"

"Of course." Prairie breathed. "This isn't you, Billy. Not a lick of it. So, you best tell me who's got you doing this."

"I can't or he'll . . ." Billy shut his eyes and shook his head like this was all just some bad dream, ". . . he's gonna kill me if he finds you here."

"Who! Who is gonna—"

A gunshot rattled Prairie down to her bones. Jumping away from Billy, her heart stopped in her chest as a high-pitched scream came from the other side of the cellar.

Chapter 25
The Shot

Marrok was on the floor, dead as a dormouse. Prairie brought her hand to her mouth, catching a guttural gasp as tears rolled down her face. His eyes were still open. Blood poured from the hole right through his forehead. Another man had already taken an inconsolable Clarabelle and dragged her past them back toward the cells. Billy kept Prairie's arm locked against him. No amount of struggling could break her free. He barely glanced at Marrok lying there, face locked like if he showed one ounce of weakness, they'd shoot him too.

"You're in real deep now, boy." A tall, bearded fella wielding the gun that surely cut Marrok down stepped toward them, pushing his weight, and casting a mean shadow. He glanced at Prairie. "Get up to the house. Take her to the office." Billy gave a silent nod and hurried up the stairs, pulling Prairie like an insubordinate dog.

Marrok. He told her he was tough to kill. Yet it only took one bullet, and he was gone.

The thought stung Prairie's heart like a hornet; the burn cut through her arteries and into her bones. She couldn't stop her teeth from rattling and her chest from heaving up and down something awful.

"They shot him . . ." she barely whispered as Billy dragged her up the stairs. ". . . they killed him."

"Prairie." Billy pulled her aside once they reached the porch steps. He looked back toward the cellar, seeing no one was directly following them. "Prairie, you listen to me, and you listen good."

She could barely focus on his sea blue eyes. This was a loose cannonball now, rolling all over the deck, trying to find which hole to fall into.

"You do whatever he says. You hear me? Don't try to be brave. You do whatever he says, and we can get out of this. I promise you. Both of us will get out of this."

She nodded, but not because she agreed. What she knew she had to do and what she wanted to do weren't the same. Her legs wanted to run as fast as the moonlight touched the trees on a summer night, but her mind wanted answers. Wanted justice, if for nothing else, for Marrok.

The house was a ghost of its former self. Most of the furniture was still shrouded in sheets that weren't the least bit white any-more. The walls, once colored with olive photographs and art, were stingy and vacant. Shadows of where the pictures once lived still clung to the walls like they were hoping they'd return one day. Dust floated through the air. Even in the corners you could see it, places where no light touched.

A solid staircase loomed in front of her before Billy pulled her to the left. This used to be the parlor room. A place for cigars and jovial banter as the women tended to the meals. Two long stretched couches sat across from one another, and a tall standing desk rested back between them.

A man was standing at that desk, a walled bookcase behind

him. Prairie's eyes fell on his familiar peppered hair, beady eyes, and crooked grin.

"Miss. O'Shea." Bernard Hemsworth puffed on his cigar like one of the New York mobsters from the movies.

The hand clutching her arm grew tighter. Prairie turned as Billy passed her off to someone else. The man, shadowed and stout, dragged her in front of the desk and forced her to her knees. She wretched her arm from him, and Bernard raised his hand to the man, indicating to him not to retaliate against her.

"I apologize if my men brought you any harm. But you must understand." He took another drag. "You've put me in a very . . . difficult position."

"I understand, Mr. Hemsworth." Prairie rubbed her arm as she met his unfeeling eyes.

"Good." He flashed his yellowing teeth before sneering at Billy. Billy stood a few feet from Prairie, shifting nervously in his stance, his fingers pressing down against his trousers.

"I told you, William." Bernard moved from behind the desk. "You spend too much time with this girl, she's gonna get caught up in all this. The kind of girl she is, she's liable to pry." He blew a puff of rancid smoke into Billy's face. "Didn't I tell you that?"

Billy swallowed hard, his throat shifting and posture stiffening. "Yes, sir."

Seeing how he spoke to Billy, and how easily his confidence was stripped from him when he stood before his uncle, turned the fear into anger. She always knew how crooked Bernard was, but this . . . this was lower than low.

"Glad you recall, my boy." Bernard patted him across the cheek. "Maybe you'll learn from this."

"Now, Miss. O'Shea." Bernard came around to stand in front of her. His stocky form leaned in his pin striped suit; his tie was perfectly adjusted around his neck.

"The last thing I want is to create any unrest in our community. Our families have known each other for a long time. I would hate to see any ill will befall your father. Word gets out about my little . . . side business I'm running here, it would look pretty bad for us. And for us I mean you and your own."

He turned to snuff his cigar into a glass ashtray on the desk. "We can forget you ever came here. Forget you saw anything in that cellar. Don't speak a word of this to anyone and all will be overlooked. I'll make sure William keeps an eye on you until I'm comfortable that you won't squeal. Not to your daddy and not to the police."

Bernard looked down on her, the corner of his mouth twitching with unsettled nerves and a hint of excitement. "I trust you to do the right thing here."

Prairie held her breath, sitting up straight as an arrow on her knees. "And what exactly is the right thing, Mr. Hemsworth? Cuz from what I can see, you're sitting on the wrong side of it."

Prairie's veins ran cold for a shake, but only a shake. The more she glared at this pig of a man, the more her blood fizzled like a shaken-up bottle of soda. She wasn't afraid of him, and she wouldn't be a pincher for anyone like him, even if it meant she'd never see her family again.

Bernard fell back against the desk and folded his arms. "You're not going to keep quiet about this, are you Miss. O'Shea?"

"No." Prairie swallowed any fear that tried to leak from her eyes, keeping herself strong. For those girls in the cellar. For Marrok. "I don't think I will."

"Even at the risk of your family's safety and your own?"

"What about the girl's safety? And their family's? Are you offering them the same as you do me?"

A low chortle rumbled inside his gut. "I thought you'd say that." He took another step. "The war may be over, but equality is an illusion. In hindsight, this country is just as bad as Germany. Only we keep it quiet. So, nobody asks questions. Except . . . someone like you."

He sighed as his chin settled against his chest to look down at her. "Shame that I'll have to deliver the grave news of your disappearance to your folks."

Prairie braced herself for what was to come. Being dragged away by her hair, stuffed in a cell with the rest of those poor souls he'd locked away, to be shipped off like birds in a cage, not knowing who or what would happen to them. She'd find a way out. No matter how long it took, she'd get free and then Bernard Hemsworth would get what's due.

She turned to Billy, who stared at her with fists clenched and his chest rising and falling like a tide coming in strong to a shore. He didn't move, didn't even speak a word. She could see the tension in his eyes, not knowing what to do. Too scared to act, even for her.

"Jim." Bernard gestured toward one of his downturned, derbyed men. He kept his hand held out, Jim glanced at it before relinquishing his piece from inside his coat pocket.

It was a pistol, catching the last rays of sun across its silver body. Prairie watched him carefully as Bernard turned to Billy, shoving it in his hand, breaking Billy's focus.

"What . . ." Billy looked from the gun to his uncle. "What's this for?"

"As I see it, this is your mistake, William." Bernard stepped back and gestured down to the kneeling Prairie. "So, you best take care of it."

"Take care of it?" Billy and Prairie's eyes locked.

Bernard walked back to his chair, falling into it with a relaxing sigh. "Get behind her." He pointed his finger, holding up his thumb and squinted. "And pull the trigger."

Chapter 26
The Massacre

Billy looked from the gun in his hand to Bernard. "What?"

"You heard me." Bernard lit another cigar. "We can't have her flapping her mouth. So, get behind her. Put the barrel to her pretty little head. And shoot her dead."

Billy watched him, his chest heaving as harsh as the wind on a stormy night. The sun was threatening to abandon them as it sank deeper behind the trees. When Billy looked at her, Prairie's eyes shuttered, holding his gaze like she wished she could keep him from moving.

Nothing was louder than the blood rushing in her ears and the mad speed of her heart breaking against her ribs. She couldn't breathe, knowing her fate was in the hands of the boy she could never bring herself to say yes to.

Billy closed his gaping mouth; determination rose into his cheeks as his grip tightened on the gun. He lifted it straight out, pointing it at Bernard, his finger trembling at the trigger. "I can't shoot her. I won't. But I sure as hell will shoot you."

Prairie's breath caught in her throat. Nobody moved; the air thick with heat. Bernard didn't seem the least bit worried. His casual eyes more sinister than a man fearing for his life or one about to take one.

"You disappoint me." Bernard gestured with a single raise of his chin as he placed his cigar on the ashtray. "Just like your father."

Jim and another man in a checkered jacket grabbed Billy's arms and twisted them behind his back. Jim ripped the gun from his struggling hands as the checkered man pushed Billy to his knees in front of Prairie. Billy hung his head with a grunt, raising his eyes to meet hers. Prairie didn't blink once as she watched Billy flood with regret.

Bernard rose from his chair, taking his cigar with him and tasting its harsh grittiness. "First, she dies. And then it's your turn." Jim came up behind her. "To think I thought I could mold you once your father was out of the picture. You should have died with them that night."

"You bastard!" Billy tried to get up, but got a swift boot to the stomach, crashing him to his knees yet again. "Don't you lay a finger on her." Hair hung across his face as he looked up to catch Prairie's gaze again. "Prairie. Prairie, I'm sorry."

There was nothing left to feel. Not for Marrok, Billy, or his folks Bernard practically confessed to killing. Prairie didn't want to die, but she also didn't want Billy to think he didn't do anything to try and stop it. "It's okay, Billy. It's okay . . . it's okay."

Cold iron penetrated her hair, rubbing against the back of her skull. Closing her eyes, Prairie tried to keep her breathing calm to stop herself from shaking. The only thought left that riddled her mind was Marrok, lying still and lifeless in the basement.

"Our Father, who art in heaven," Tears touched her freckled cheeks. "Hallowed be thy name."

"Prairie . . ." Desperation coursed through Billy's voice as he called her name.

"Thy kingdom come, thy will be done, on Earth as it is in heaven."

"Last chance to reconsider." Bernard's voice shot open her

eyes. Prairie hardened her stare, straightening her back as her chest heaved.

"Give us this day our daily bread and forgive us our trespasses. As we forgive those who trespass against us."

Bernard tapped his cigar on the ashtray. "Have it your way."

Her voice grew louder. "And lead us not into temptation but deliver us from evil."

Bernard nodded and the gun clicked to ready itself.

"For thine is the kingdom . . . and the power . . ."

Billy gritted his teeth. "Prairie, *no!*"

"And the glory, now . . . and forever—"

Splintered wood and sheetrock exploded around them, covering the room with shards of chaos. The gun shifted, going off to the right of her. A sharp ringing collapsed Prairie to the floor as rubble rained down on top of her. Men scrambled, shooting off their guns left and right. Prairie was barely able to drag her now free hands to her ears. Her head was spinning, unable to focus. Someone grabbed her arms and dragged her across the floor to the far-left corner of the room.

The ringing muffled any sound coming in, but the hands that grabbed her came to her face, distracting her from the bleeding pain pounding her head like a mallet.

"Prairie . . . *Prairie!*" Billy shouted at her. His face was covered in dust and debris. He only focused on her for a second, before shoving her against the wall, shielding her from the chaos beating through the room.

Prairie looked up over his shoulder, her eyes widening at the scene unfolding in front of them.

There he was, jet black fur and pointed teeth, ripping through the panicked men like a knife slicing through watermelon. His towering body took bullet after bullet, all cutting through him, but failing to stop the slaughter. Hulking arms picked up men and threw them clean through the wall, snarling like the mad dog he was.

Prairie caught the soft brown of his eyes and, for a split second, Marrok tensed. Clamoring feet down the stairs were barely an echo as Marrok launched himself toward them. Billy shuttered, closing his eyes as he pressed Prairie to the wall, but fear didn't grip her now. Slipping out from under him, Prairie stood on wavering legs as Marrok breathed his blood-stained musk over her face, baring his ugly teeth.

"No!" She lifted her hand and placed it on the muscled arch of his heaving coat. "You promised me!" Marrok sneered, ears pricked. Footsteps charged into the room as more guns shot in their direction. Prairie ducked just in time for Marrok to make short work of the newcomers' attempts to stop him.

Grabbing Billy by the arms, she wretched him to stand. "Come on, Billy. Get up." Billy stared into her eyes, shifting, and scared like a cat in the rain.

"*Billy.*" Prairie tried to ignore the screams and gurgling breaths of the men being cut though behind her as she bent down to him. "We need to get out of here!"

A gun cocked close to her head. Prairie froze, the glint of a barrel appearing in her sight. Marrok's manic onslaught suddenly ceased and all was quiet, except for his deep, heaving breath.

"Get up, you." Bernard's stern voice cut through her still ringing ears. Prairie rose to her feet. "Now, turn around."

Dragging her foot back, she raised her hands as she turned. Everything was painted with blood. Bodies were strewn about the room, some without arms or legs. Throats ripped and eyes transfixed. All the furniture broke and splintered, mimicking the men who once used them for their means. The smell of iron suffocated the room, making her nose scrunch and her eyes bleed with tears.

Bernard pushed the gun into the back of her skull, forcing her to take a few weary steps forward. She could feel her stomach wrench from the heavy scent in the air. Parts not meant to be seen, laid bare in the light of the moon.

Her eyes finally met Marrok. His chest heaved as blood-drenched saliva dripped from his terrible fangs. A low grumble threatened to set loose the monster once again, but he remained poised. Carefully watching as Bernard's ugly disheveled smirk coated his face.

Chapter 27
The Sacrifice

"Well," Bernard laughed nervously. "Seems like I have something you want."

Prairie could feel the gun trembling in his hand, but she wasn't stupid enough to try and get away. Not with his finger so tight on the trigger.

"So, you're the one who's been killing my men." Bernard breathed. Marrok snarled in response, his clawed feet sliding across the blood-soaked floor.

"Not another step . . . or I'll empty my gun right in this pretty girl's head."

Marrok stopped. The sharp instruments of his gnarled hands flexing where he stood.

"Now, you let me go . . .." Bernard's breath was short. "An' maybe. Maybe I'll let her live."

He shoved Prairie toward the broken wall where Marrok first burst in from.

"Move along, Prairie."

Her heart never beat so fast, each step rummaging through the carnage of the scene. The floor was slick with blood. Every few inches her white kicks would squish and slide along its surface.

Bernard fell close behind her, turning to stay in the foreground as they stood just outside his planned escape.

"There we are." He muttered through his teeth. Marrok snarled again. His lip reached the topmost fold of his narrow snout, eyes glinting with anticipation.

"I'd love to stay, but it's time to say . . . goodbye." Bernard clicked the gun.

She closed her eyes as she felt the tension just before the pull. Prairie dropped to the floor.

A scuffle behind her opened her eyes, not knowing why she was still breathing. Blood soaked the base of her uniform, slowly crawling down her leg and mixing with the red of the already stained floor.

Billy wrestled with Bernard, desperately grabbing at the gun, and trying to wretch it free. With a solid arm, Bernard shoved Billy clean across the room. He dragged himself through the wall on his back. Prairie pushed up on her arms, turning to see the gun wavering in Bernard's hand. He found his aim and pointed the gun at her just before his eyes glazed, following the shadow that crept over her before it swallowed him whole.

Prairie ducked as the gun went off again, hearing Bernard's wretched scream cut through the night as Marrok quickly ended his life in the worst possible way. Her heart pounded, lungs rising and falling so fast she thought she might never open her eyes again. Crunching and sputtering suffocated her ears. She tried not to listen, keeping her eyes shut tight, afraid to witness what she knew was happening just behind her.

She didn't know how long she sat there before a hand touched her back. Kind, soul-filled eyes fell into her view, a round moon scar on his midnight skin.

"Marrok."

He wore sullied slacks that didn't belong to him. His chest exposed, dotted with so many bullet holes and scars, Prairie couldn't begin to count. Some were closing right before her eyes, stopping the flow of blood.

She tried to sit up but fell back to the floor. Marrok gathered her up, leaned her against the wall and pulled the skirt up of her red, stained uniform. It was almost like a rain-filled cloud, too heavy to hold on, burst from her thigh. Her mind went fuzzy seeing all that blood pouring out of her. Marrok ripped a long train of cloth from a dead man's shirt and quickly tied it just above the bullet hole, pulling so hard she thought it cut right through to her bone.

Billy stood behind him and watched, frozen in unbelievable fright. Marrok glanced over his shoulder before continuing to try and stop the bleeding. "There a phone here?" He spoke so calmly, you'd think they weren't sitting in a room that had just been torn to pieces.

Marrok looked at him again. "A phone."

His words shocked Billy awake. He nodded his head.

"Call the police." Marrok waited for him to act, but Billy just stood there, slack-jawed. "Call the damn cops, *now!*"

Billy jumped to life, rushing out of the room without taking the time to notice the parts he was tripping over.

"Marrok." Prairie winched as he put pressure on the wound. "Marrok."

"Got to try and stop the bleeding." He said quietly. He was covered in blood and all the things he ripped from this room.

Prairie swallowed, squinting to keep herself awake before shaking the cobwebs from her eyes. "*Marrok.*" The sudden stern-ness drew his focus to her." You gotta get outta here."

"I ain't leavin' ya like this."

"You have to. You can't be here."

Billy ran back into the room. "They're coming." He dropped beside Marrok. "Let me help. Please."

Caution flashed in Marrok's eyes, but he let Billy's hands fall to her thigh. Prairie took Marrok's hands, ignoring how soaked they were with her own blood and pulled him closer with all her strength.

"It's done now." She swallowed back the pain. "They can't . . ." She gripped his hand tighter. ". . . You can't let them find you." Tears start rolling down her sullied face. "I thought you were dead."

"I told you." He managed a weak smile. "It's pretty damn hard to kill me." He reached his hands to cup her face, his mouth falling open to words he didn't wish to speak. "I'll come back. I'll come home."

"You better."

The whole world could have been watching and it wouldn't have mattered a lick. Marrok captured her lips, the threads of passion weaved between them would bring any girl to their knees. It lasted for more than she deserved and less than she wanted, making her forget the throbbing life escaping through a bullet hole in her thigh. They breathed into each other before he parted, leaving the freckles of her cheeks burning with the fiery sparks of her heart.

She gripped on to his wrist, not wanting him to go but knowing his fate if he stayed. Marrok kissed her forehead before letting her hand slip from his arm. As quickly as he stood, he was gone, running out into the night as the stars flickered through the trees.

Prairie leaned back against the wall. Billy looked at her, misunderstanding no longer evident in his face. She dropped her hand on his, still trying to relieve the bleeding.

"Thank you." She said softly.

"No." The sound of sirens grew in the distance. "This is my fault. I didn't do anything right."

"You did." She squeezed his hand as cobwebs began to crawl in front of her eyes again. "You did."

They waited together until the flashing red and blue lights

landed on the front porch. Badges fell on the scene, but Prairie didn't last much longer, letting the loss of blood lull her into deep, quiet darkness.

177

Chapter 28
The Promise

The bullet had gone clean through. Prairie's head throbbed from exhaustion, but closing her eyes wasn't an option either. The stain of death still lingered on her mind. All that blood and those broken bodies. She didn't think she'd ever be rid of it. The only thing keeping her from slipping back into the fear was the constant beeping of the heart monitor by her bedside and the taste of Marrok's last kiss lingering on her lips.

"You lost a lot of blood." The dark-haired doctor stated as he pushed up his specks. "We'll keep an eye on you for the next few days."

Billy sat in the chair beside the bed, hands folded as he leaned down on his knees. He looked okay, aside from some bumps and bruises.

"Your parents are on their way. Just rest now. We'll let you know when they arrive."

"Thank you." Prairie spoke quietly as the doctor nodded and left the room.

They sat in silence together. Prairie's leg throbbed underneath the bandages and stitching. It would be a while until she would be able to walk properly again. The muscles in her leg needed time to recover from having a bullet rip a hole in her. A slight ringing in her ears from the gun that went off by her head still lingered, but not bad enough that she couldn't hear a lick.

Billy sniffed loudly, wiping his hand across his nose. Prairie tried to sit up but winched from the pain shooting up her leg and into her back. "Did the cops talk to you?"

He shook his head. "No."

Prairie let out a long, drawn-out breath as she sank into the bed. "What are they waiting for?"

"Excuse me." They both looked toward the door as Detective Greenway poked his sullen face in. "Might I have a word?"

Prairie's back tensed as he stepped in, closing the door behind him. Billy sat up as Greenway walked to the foot of the bed, adjusting his tan trench coat. He was carrying a briefcase, which he laid on the movable high tray that was left there. His hand went to his inside pocket as he relinquished his leather badge holder.

"I already know who you are, Detective." Prairie stated quietly.

"I think a more formal introduction is in order." He opened it, but instead of the NYPD letters popping out in black, there were others that Prairie didn't recognize.

"I'm an investigator with the Bureau of Supernatural Affairs—or BOSA." He returned his ID to his inside pocket. "We received information that a supernatural entity had been spotted in this area a few months ago."

He proceeded to open his briefcase. A manilla folder came into his hand, which he opened and moved across the bed. "A man by the name of James Buchanan."

Prairie took the folder and dragged it onto her lap. Marrok's picture was paper-clipped to the front of a stack, documenting his physical description and a slew of sightings, including events and attempts at apprehension. Her hand came up to cover her mouth as Billy leaned in to garner a look for himself.

"You might know him by another name." Prairie looked up at Greenway as he spoke.

"Marrok." She breathed.

Billy took the file and sifted through the papers. "What does all this mean?"

"I've been tracking Mr. Buchanan and his activities across the US for a number of years now. He's been an entity of interest to us but impossible to secure. When his MO matched the murders on your stretch of highway, I knew it was only a matter of time before we ran into him. But you . . . well, you got to him first."

"What do you want with him?" Billy asked.

Greenway held his hands behind his back. "It's the bureau's responsibility to apprehend and regulate the activities of all supernatural beings in this country. A werewolf, like Mr. Buchanan, left unchecked, is dangerous."

Prairie remained still as he spoke, though her thoughts were practically leaking from her ears. Every so often, she glanced at Billy, who seemed to be taking it all in with quiet concentration.

"We are familiar with his mission, but you must understand, we don't need any unnecessary attention brought on by his actions. It is our job to keep the citizens of this country safe and their lives uninterrupted as much as possible. If a discovery of this sort were to leak to the public, the consequences could be catastrophic."

He took the file from Billy and placed it back into his briefcase. "When I discovered, you, Miss. O'Shea, were involved in some way, I took it upon myself to keep tabs on you. So, I must ask." He clicked the briefcase closed. "Do you know where he may have fled to?"

Prairie shook her head, keeping her lips taught. "No. I just told him to go."

"Are you sure?"

"She said she doesn't know." Billy's voice raised. "I was sitting right there with her when she said it."

Prairie's eyes flashed to Billy in his defense of her. He looked at her reassuringly before facing Greenway again.

The detective curled his lips. "I see." He dragged the briefcase across the table, clutching it in his hand. "We don't intend to harm Mr. Buchanan. The safety of all supernatural entities is just as important to us as any other. But the longer he is out there without the protection of the Bureau, the more in danger he is of becoming a target."

He took a card out of his pocket and handed it to Billy, who took it from him without question. "If you hear anything, this is where you can reach me." He proceeded to walk toward the door.

"Wait." Billy stood. "What happens now? What about all them dead at the cabin?"

Greenway turned to face them. "Law enforcement has been briefed and any corrections that need to be made have already been taken care of. The Bureau knows how to cover its tracks, Mr. Hemsworth." He shifted his gaze from Billy to Prairie. "I trust I don't need to send either of you to corrections?"

"Corrections?" Billy asked.

"Usually when civilians are involved in supernatural cases, they are sent to have their memories altered. But I can tell by your . . . closeness to this individual," he straightened his posture, "that it will not be an issue?"

Billy clenched his teeth, looking at Prairie who watched him with a careful gaze. She tensed, not knowing what Billy would say. She wouldn't say anything, but Billy, didn't have a reason to lie.

"Who would believe us anyway." His words flooded Prairie's face with a relieving sigh.

Billy looked back to Greenway. "Nobody will hear about it. Now that it's over."

"Good." Greenway gave a single nod. "I won't take up any

more of your time. You have my card." He turned the handle and walked through the door, then closed it with a click.

Billy's fists tightened at his sides as he turned himself to face Prairie. "You love that monster?"

"He's not a monster." She folded her hands briefly before cutting her frustration short.

"He's just a man. Like you, or daddy, or anybody." The tension from his words quickly dissipated.

"You really won't say anything about what happened?"

"No." Billy sat back down in the chair. "No, I won't say anything."

Prairie relaxed. "Thank you." She let the silence swallow the room for a moment, trying to process everything that had happened. The lines between reality and fairy tale all blurred together. If there was an entire government department dedicated to overseeing people like Marrok, what other impossibilities were not impossible at all? That Greenway didn't force them to have their memories corrected was a ploy, because he hoped Marrok would come back.

Prairie looked up at the pale ceiling. "What's gonna happen now?" Her head rolled to Billy, who sat in quiet contemplation. "You're all that's left of your family, Billy."

His gaze wandered up to her forest green eyes. "I know. And I've got to make it better. Somehow. I got to atone for what happened. Help the cops in any way I can, even if it means I get locked up for it." He pulled the chair forward, gingerly taking Prairie's hand in his. "But first thing I'm gonna do, I'm gonna pay for your nursing school."

Prairie's eyes widened. "Billy, you don't have to do that."

"No, I do. And I won't take no for an answer. From you or your folks." He straightened his posture. "You never accepted the bad in me, Prairie. Only the good. And I've been fighting to keep it locked away because that's what my uncle wanted. When he told me to kill you, I ... I knew I couldn't just be a bystander anymore. I had to stand up to that piece of trash once and for all. For you and all those he'd hurt. Even if I died trying. I never want to be that helpless again."

"Billy Hemsworth." Prairie sighed, shaking her head as she touched down on their connection. "I . . . don't know what to say."

"Say the one thing you could never say to me." His charming grin overtook him as her gaze came back to him. "Say yes, and I promise you, I'll be better. Then maybe one day, you can say yes to me more." He moved to the edge of his seat. "You're it for me, Prairie. Nothing made me realize that more than watching you in that room, standing up to my uncle while still trying to save me. You're . . . the strongest person I've ever known, with the bravest, most beautiful heart a person could have."

She squeezed his hand, trying to keep her composure. "He killed your father. Your mother." He looked down at their hands, carefully turning hers over in his.

"You know, you'd think I'd be more shaken up by that. Knowing he was behind it." He expelled a drawn-out sight. "Maybe part of me always knew. The part that wanted to be like him. The part that accepted that I had to do bad things to get ahead." He looked up at her, "Am I a terrible person for thinking that?"

Prairie's teeth came down on the inside of her lips. "I don't know, Billy. But I hope to God you don't want to be that person anymore."

"No . . . I don't ever want to be like him. I don't need to be. Not when I got you. Something he never had, and it made him a monster worse than your werewolf." She smiled at the sudden change in him. He was bright again, that glint returning with a new purpose. New ambitions swam in his hopeful eyes that made her heart flutter. The only good thing she'd felt lying in that hospital bed.

"You're going to nursing school. And I'll make things right. For everyone I've hurt. And for all those still hurting."

Chapter 29
The Lincoln

Billy spared no expense when it came to chauffeuring, but it wasn't Billy driving. After cleaning up what his uncle left behind and cooperating with authorities to get those taken returned to their families, Billy was the head of Hemsworth Manufacturing. It was seeing more success than even he could have imagined. Not only that, but he also personally headed and constructed the first unsegregated community hospital in the entire state of New York.

Prairie sat in the backseat of the spacious Lincoln, dressed head to toe in her white nursing uniform. Billy sat beside her, dressed in a finely pressed suit and tie. His hair was slicked and face cleanly shaven with an arm resting across Prairie's shoulders. The smoke from his cigarette gently escaped out of the crack in the window.

A lot had changed in three years, and most of it was unexpected.

"I'll have Ben pick you up tomorrow afternoon from the hospital." Billy smirked as she turned to meet his gaze.

"You don't need to send Ben. I can manage."

"I know you'd rather take a cab, but tomorrow's special."

She grinned teasingly as she leaned back against the door. "And what's so special about it?"

Billy leaned close to her. "If I tell you, it won't be a surprise now, will it?"

Their noses touched, leaking a soft sigh from her lips. "I'm not a girl who likes surprises."

"This one, I think you'll like."

Billy offered up a smooth, sensual kiss across her pale red lips. She still had a hard time believing this was her life. Head Nurse of the recovery ward at the Hemsworth Community Hospital. And Billy: he became a man of respect and selfless honesty. And he loved her, ever so much. Prairie closed her eyes, allowing herself to get lost in the dull taste of tobacco on his tongue before he gently parted from her.

"We're here, ma'am." The driver, Ben, said as he pulled up to the entrance of the hospital.

Prairie slipped her hand under his arm and relinquished herself from him. "I'll see you tomorrow."

"I'll be counting down the minutes."

With a smile, she opened the door and slipped out. "I bet you will." Before she left, she leaned in and planted another sweet kiss goodbye on his lips. "Don't work too hard now."

Billy smiled as she shut the door, watching the Lincoln pull around the parking lot and out of sight.

Prairie waited in the morning sun, listening to the wind rattle through the autumn leaves. She opened the lip of her purse, and pulled out a white handkerchief, rubbing it between her fingers as she brought it to her nose to take in the weak scent of turned earth and coffee.

It was the times between distractions that her mind wandered. Back to the dimly lit dive bar and the sound of her voice over the microphone. To Marrok's subtle touch, the scent of black coffee seeping through her nostrils as he carried her onto the dance floor. To that kiss before disappearing into the night. If she closed her eyes long enough, she could see him. That James Dean smoothness carried him in his stride like music on the wind. The plump feel of his lips on hers, taking in the bitter taste of love.

It had been three years since he'd left. Three years of hoping and praying he'd return to her. But he never did. Not a call or a letter. Nothing. She held on for longer than she needed to but less than she wanted. He was an unmatched man who sunk his teeth into her heart from the moment she laid eyes on him. Even remembering him at his worst, the carnage he could inflict and the fear he could awake inside a person, sent her heart racing.

It was the not knowing that kept her in one place for so long. But she couldn't hold on anymore. Not like she was. It was too painful. So, she tried to move on. With Billy. And she was trying to love him like she did Marrok. She did love Billy, but it wasn't *true* love, no matter how much she wanted to make it true. It was a constant feeling she kept reminding herself to ignore, so she could just be happy with what she had. And she was happy, most of the time. Billy was a man worth being happy for, even if it meant she could never know true love's kiss again.

Chapter 30
The Visitor

“There's a new patient in room six, Prairie.” Molly looked up from the desk, her blonde hair pinned up tight in a bun underneath her cap. She slid over the clipboard to her. “Special request.”

The hospital was bustling this evening, the waiting room already filled with people looking to be seen. A gentle mix of white and colored alike.

“Thanks, Molly.” Prairie took the clipboard and scanned it. “Broken arm from a fall?”

“Doctors already set it. And bandages need to be restocked there, last time it was checked.”

“I'll grab some before going in.”

Molly grinned. “The patient requested you. Said he heard about you.”

Prairie scoffed, running her hand down her white pleated uniform. “I'm sure I treated a relative, is all.”

“Mmm hmm.” Molly smirked. “You sure you ain't playing? Best not tell Mr. Hemsworth his girl is loose on the patients now.”

“Billy knows I'm a one-man kinda girl.”

“Look at you, showing off. You're the only one who can call

him by his first name 'round here. He's so sweet on you it burns my taste buds."

Prairie smiled and turned from the desk. "Get back to work, Molly."

She leaned an elbow on the desk. "Don't you got a date with him tomorrow?"

"That's not your business!" Prairie couldn't help but smile as she pushed through the doors to the patient rooms.

Her white sneakers squeaked across the floor. She greeted her fellow nurses and a few doctors who nodded their heads as she walked by.

Fishing the keys from her pocket, she reached the storage closet and slipped it into the lock. It clicked as she turned the knob and pressed the door open, kicking the door stand down so it wouldn't close all the way and lock her in. The metal shelving reached a foot or two before the ceiling.

Prairie flipped the light switch and stepped to the left where the bandages were housed. She pulled a few rolls from the shelf, along with gauze and a box of cotton balls. Scanning the shelf, she took a step to her right and perked up on her toes to reach a brown bottle of iodine.

When she came down, she turned back toward the door, only for her heart to jump out of her chest. Everything she'd collected dropped from her hands between her and the man standing in front of her. His perfume hit her like a snowball on a cold winter day, earth mixed with the strong scent of dark coffee.

"Marrok." His name fell from her lips as the iodine spread across the linoleum floor.

Marrok stood there like he'd always had. A gray undershirt poking out from between his unbuttoned jean jacket. His hair was the same, maybe a little longer, but still perfectly slicked to compliment his proud nose and distinguished jaw.

He watched her with deep, careful eyes. "You're lookin' well."

"I . . ." she swallowed. ". . . I didn't think I'd ever see you again."

Marrok stepped forward, drawing closer to her. He moved as smoothly as she remembered.

"I said I'd come back for ya. It took me longer than I was expecting but . . . I'm here now."

Prairie squeezed her hands together, not sure if she should be elated or angry, seeing him here now. "What took you so long?"

Marrok bit his lip and looked away from her, holding in a breath before letting it vent from his partially opened mouth. "A lot of things. The fuzz, mostly. People needing me elsewhere." He came back to her. "I couldn't write or call. It was too dangerous, and I knew them bureau fellas were just waiting for me to come to ya."

"I see." Her chin dropped to her chest. It made sense, his reasonings for not coming sooner. But surely, he could have done something. Anything. If only to let her know he was alive. And that he hadn't forgotten about her. "You didn't come here just to see me, Marrok."

"No," He sighed. "I didn't just come to see you." His boots touched gingerly across the floor as he glanced down at them. Prairie watched his hands twitch before his thumbs hooked in his pockets. "I'm here to ask . . . if you'd come with me."

Footsteps echoed down the hall. Marrok didn't hesitate in placing his hands on her shoulders, pulling her from the shelf and against the wall next to the door. Prairie moved her palms to his chest and kept them there. Her heart was beating like thunder, her hands sweating against the cotton of his shirt. She was sure she was shaking or perhaps he was. He smelled like a fresh brewed cup of joe, no sugar. Bitter. Just the bite you'd need to wake up.

She could feel the drum inside his chest, pounding something awful as he cast his gaze down to her. Prairie folded her lips as she pressed as hard as she could into the wall. The footsteps came and went in a blink, but they remained there, looking into each other's eyes, unable to pull themselves away.

Prairie held her breath as Marrok's hands eased off her shoulders before taking a step back. A rush of air escaped his flaring nostrils as she eased from the wall. She reached for her arm, holding on tight to collect herself. She never wanted to kiss a man so bad. Like if she denied herself, she just might fall over dead. But she couldn't and clearly, he couldn't either. Not until what needed to be said was said.

"Marrok . . ."

"I know it's a lot to ask." His tone dropped a wink. "You've been working hard and it ain't fair for me to ask you to walk away from all this." His shifting eyes settled on her with a single breath. "I've told you before, I ain't a selfish man."

There was nothing keeping her from going to him, letting him take her in his arms and never letting her go. She wanted to, so badly it hurt, but she couldn't allow herself to fall. Not this time.

Prairie closed her eyes, balling her fists at her sides, and finally allowing herself to breathe. "I waited for you. I waited for three years. Hoping . . ." She opened her eyes, letting the pressure rise deep within her bones.

". . . I'd see you outside my window at night. That your Thunderbird would cruise up the road as I walked. I thought about you all the time. Asking God to keep you safe. To let me see you again. Tomorrow. And the tomorrow after that. But you never came, and I couldn't wait anymore."

Marrok swallowed, twisting his mouth into a knot as he focused on the door. "I tried to leave it alone. After so long, I tried. Knowin' you probably moved on and I didn't wanna be the one to disrupt your life again." He looked at her.

"But you're all I dream about. All I think of. Every moment

we've shared replayed in my mind like a record skipping in a juke-box. I can't shake you, Prairie. I don't think I'm meant to."

Prairie took a hasty step toward him before stopping herself. "So, you think, after all this time, I'm just gonna drop everything I've done and come with you? Is that what you think?"

"No. I don't think that."

Her muscles tensed, tightening her back and twisting her neck as she tried to hold back tears. "I got a life here, Marrok. A purpose. I got . . . a boy who became the man I always knew he could be." Anger mixed with uncertainty, dragging down her face. "He says he did it for me, even though I never asked him to. He . . . loves me."

"Prairie—"

"I'm not done talking." She snapped, stuffing a whimper down her throat that ceased her stomach. "You think this is a simple ask with a simple answer?"

Tension riddled Marrok's face, flexing the scar on his left cheek. "It's not."

"No, you're wrong." Her lip began to tremble. "It is."

Her hand came to clutch the open collar of her uniform. "Cuz the moment you said it, all I wanted to do was fall into your arms and never leave." She paused, shutting her eyes. "Every time I'm not . . . distracting myself with work or Billy, all I think about . . . is you. And I . . . curse myself for it. For refusing to let you go. For not being able to love Billy like he loves me. And now you're here and it feels like," her voice shook as she dared to look at him gain.

"It feels like that night I danced with you, my heart jumping out of my chest. So fresh in my mind I can still feel your arm around my waist and . . . remember how you looked at me. Like I was the only thing that mattered."

His shoulders sank his entire frame. It was the first time she'd ever see him look so defeated. "I'm sorry for coming back. But I had to know. I had to try. If I didn't, I'd regret it for the rest of my life."

"I'm glad you came back." She nodded, shaking more loose tears to the floor. "That you're okay. That you're alive. I thought . . ." Another breath caught in her throat. ". . . For so long I thought you were dead. That was the only reason I could think of for you not coming back to me."

Silence filled the storage room as they both watched each other. Prairie's green eyes flickered steadily on the pools of brown she would willingly swim through again. But there was too much hurt right now. She couldn't think straight. And she'd be losing so much. She needed time, even though she knew it would be short.

"I'm leaving town the day after tomorrow." He said calmly. "I can't stay in one place too long."

"Two days," she scoffed with a sniff. "Only two days to decide the rest of my life."

"Whatever you decide. I'll respect it—the choice you make." His lips tensed, "You'll never see me again."

"Already decided for me?" Prairie dropped her hand. "You know better."

"Maybe I don't."

Prairie backed toward the door, never letting him leave her gaze. He watched her, his usual cool confidence now shaken up something terrible. Carefully, he bent down and collected the items she had dropped, presenting them to her slowly. It took everything in her not to reach for him. To let her hand fall to his face and recount the memory of his kiss.

She took everything from him, holding it tight against her chest as she slid into the gap between the door frame. The heaviness of what he was asking started to sink in. She could feel her knees weaken and her heart begging her to answer the call.

"Shut the door when you leave." She didn't wait for a rebuttal as she bolted from the room, walking without being fast enough to call a run. She kept her head down to avoid anyone seeing the sadness plaguing her eyes, but when she reached the desk, she couldn't avoid Molly's concern.

"Prairie, honey." She reached out a hand. "What's the matter?"

"Nothing." She sighed, sucking down her emotion as she laid the items she'd collected on the counter. "Assign another nurse to room 6, would you? I'm not feeling too well."

"Of course." Molly took the clipboard, offering her a tissue. "Are you sure nothing happened?"

"No." Prairie took the tissue and wiped the dampness from her eyes. "No, I'll be fine." She looked at Molly and forced a smile. "Thank you, Molly."

She left the desk, her heart and mind growing heavier with every stride. There was no answer that she could give where someone wasn't left in the bitter cold. That she was the one who had to make that decision, it was too much. What was right could be wrong, and what was wrong could certainly be right.

She would spend the next eight hours of her shift lost in the fog of what Marrok asked her to do, hoping something would give her the answer she couldn't bring herself to find.

Chapter 31
The Ring

No amount of lipstick and carefully pinned hair could shake Marrok from her mind. Sitting at the table of one of the finest restaurants in town, Prairie tried to enjoy herself across from a man who had given her more than she'd ever asked for.

"Prairie." Billy's voice cut through her thoughts. "Something on your mind?"

She leaned on her elbows. The candle flickering between them, reflecting in their wine glasses. "What makes you say that?"

"You're quiet. Too quiet. And you haven't been able to look at me straight." He took her hand and brought it down onto the table. "You can tell me anything. You know that."

"I know." She pulled her hand out from under his, letting it fall in the lap of her sparkling champagne dress. "Something happened at the hospital." She looked up at his expecting gaze. "Someone . . ."

Billy sat a minute before folding his hands in front of him. "Marrok." He spoke. "He came back." His gaze dropped to the floor away from the table. "I thought he'd never come back."

"It's been so long." Prairie rubbed her hands together, feeling her nerves across her palms. "Three years and he just shows up, out of the blue. He asked me . . . to go with him."

"And what did you say?" The immediate need for an answer rattled Prairie something terrible.

Shaking her head, she gazed into his hopeful yet sullen blue eyes. "I said I needed time to think. I . . . couldn't give him an answer."

They sat in silence for a while, the strings of the quartet drawing out the tense nature of their conversation. The longer they sat there, the more Prairie tossed between a comfortable life with Billy and an uncertain one with Marrok.

Drawing his hands in, Billy pushed back his well combed hair. "Well, if he's cookin with gas, I suppose I should too."

He got up, fishing in his pocket as he came around to her. Bending on one knee, he relinquished a small velvet box and let it rest in the palm of his hand. Prairie's heart stopped as he took her hand and stared longingly into her forest green eyes.

"I was hoping this would be more romantic, after a few glasses of wine, some laughs and a dance, but I can't afford to wait." He opened the box. A stunning diamond ring sat nestled in the soft pale cushion, reflecting its meaning and commitment into her eyes. Billy watched as her mouth came open, unable to speak as his promise waited for her answer.

"I can give you a comfortable life, Prairie." Billy said. "I won't ever ask you to stop working. Never expect you to wait on me hand and foot like wives are supposed to. I'll love you every day I wake up next to you. Give you a family, if that's what you want. You'll never have to worry about anything for as long as you live."

Prairie clutched her chest. "William Hemsworth." She whispered. "You know you could have any girl."

"I don't want any girl." He raised to cup her face, gently caressing her cheek. "I told you before, you're the only one." A harsh exhale escaped his nostrils.

"What kind of life would you have with him? Always running.

Never knowing where you'll end up next. Never knowing if he'd come back after a night of ripping people limb from limb."

He rested his ring bearing hand in her lap. "The world is a cruel place, Prairie. Crueler still for a white girl and a colored man. Things are starting to change, but not fast enough. I love you, that I've made clear as day."

He sighed and drew his gaze, if only to erase that dreadful thought from his mind. "You made me a better man. A better human being. And that's something I can only repay with this promise to never leave your side." More tears cascaded from her eyes. Billy settled in front of her, searching for her answer without words.

"Marry me, Prairie O'Shea."

If it were any other day, she would jump into his arms and kiss him till the sun came up. Because what Billy said was true. Any girl would be crazy to say anything but yes. Yes, to the life he offered and to the love he kept only for her.

She never saw her life fork in such opposite directions. Was what he promised her worth losing the only real love she'd ever known? And was that love worth sacrificing for a life without danger and uncertainty. With a man she could never quite bring herself to get lost in love with? To fully entwine herself with everything he was and would become?

Prairie looked down at the ring as Billy waited for her answer. An answer she'd be a fool not to give.

Chapter 32
The Heart

He stood, cool and classy, leaning against his motorcycle with a smoke stick hanging from his mouth. His hands were shoved in the pockets of his jeans jacket, and his eyes fixed on the waning sun as it dipped in the sky.

Prairie skidded her white nursing shoes in the gravel of the lot, holding onto her bag as he moved to meet her gaze. She wasn't sure if she'd find him here, but there he was.

He plucked the cigarette from his mouth, letting the smoke filter from his chimney as he threw it to the ground to snuff it out. "I didn't think I'd see you." His head tilted, watching her with careful eyes.

Prairie shrugged. "I didn't know if I would come."

"Here to say goodbye then?"

"Since when do you put words in my mouth, Marrok?" Prairie took a step, goose pimples littering every inch of her skin. "There isn't an easy way to say this."

Her lips turned in as she bit down on her words. "But the way I see things, there's an easy road and a hard road." A smile caught across her freckled cheeks. "You already know what kind of girl I am, Marrok. I'm not one to take the easy road."

He kept his unblinking gaze on her, giving her the space and

time to shed the truth that fueled her heart. As much as she had everything she ever wanted—her dreams of becoming a nurse and a man who loved her—none of it was right. She didn't carve her own way; it was carved for her. But when she was with Marrok, fighting for what she believed in without letting anyone tell her no, she was whole. She was who she was always meant to be, with the one person who let her take the first step all on her own.

"Billy asked me to marry him, and any woman in their right mind would have said yes. But I couldn't, because it doesn't feel right. My heart doesn't belong to him. It never has. Maybe moving on, maybe it was all a dream. Cuz I can't say yes and wake up every day knowing the truth. I couldn't live with myself. I'm not someone capable of living a lie."

He waited, the lines of his jaw hardening in an attempt to mask the fleeting look in his eyes. One that told her as much as he expected nothing, he hoped like hell he wouldn't regret being selfish, just this once. "An' what's your truth, Prairie?"

Prairie held her breath as the ties between them grew taut. "The truth is, I gave you my heart that very morning you walked into my diner." Her feet took her a step or two more, not allowing her focus to sway. "You left with it and . . . I haven't wanted it back since. I'd be a fool to let you keep it without me. To carry it with you while I'm carrying yours."

She came to a stop a stone's throw away. "I don't care what you are, Marrok. What color your skin is or what . . . creature you are underneath it all. Cuz I love every part of you. And I always will. 'Til I'm dead and cold in the ground."

Marrok tilted his head as his smooth stride inched him a hair closer. "I don't know, Prairie." He looked down as the tips of his boots graced her shoes. "I just don't know."

She tensed, never considering he might deny her, "Know what?"

With a calming sigh, he reached for her face, his fingers softly caressing her speckled cheek. "I don't know what I've done to deserve you."

She leaned into his palm, closing her eyes as she bathed in the feel of his touch. She grasped his arm, drawing herself toward him as his hand slid to catch the back of her neck. Her eyes came open to dive into the pools of his soft, baby browns.

He traced her jawline with his thumb. "Love ain't a big enough word. No word is."

"But it's the only word you've got."

Marrok's light breath escaped his charming smile. "I'm mad for you, Prairie O'Shea. So mad no medicine can hope to cure me of it. Though I wouldn't wanna be, even if there was."

Rising on her toes, her hands slid over the cotton of his shirt. "You better kiss me now, Marrok."

"I aim to. And every minute and every day that comes after." Tilting her back, the kiss he offered her was even more meaningful than any ring money could buy. It was a promise never to be broken by society. Even if they couldn't accept it, that didn't make it wrong. If anything, it made it right. So right, no one would understand how right it was.

When she could finally breathe again, Marrok pressed his forehead to hers. A deep sigh bringing his sweet perfume to flood her senses. "I'll never leave you again."

"I'll hold you to that." She clutched onto the edge of his jacket, pulling him into her.

"An' I'll marry you, good and proper. One day. But we can't stay too long. Not here." A gentle press of his lips on hers filled her with so much more than love. It was purpose and a sense that this was the right path for her to tread—hand in hand with her destiny.

Marrok slid down her arm and took her hand. "You ready?"

She smiled, loosening her hold on his jacket as she lost herself in his eyes. "I've been ready."

They came to his motorcycle. Marrok picked her up and placed her on the back with care. He draped his jacket across her back. Prairie slipped her arms through it as he threw his leg over the seat in front of her. She leaned against him, closing her eyes to the dream she was living.

"Hold on tight." He said as he slid his shades over his eyes. Prairie engulfed him in her arms. He kicked the engine to life as his hands twisted the throttle before sailing them into the night.

Chapter 33
The Snitch

"We're tight on the budget." One of the board members stated. "I don't think we can pull any more strings with the stockholders." The man adjusted his specs, furrowing his wrinkled brow as he lifted his gaze toward the chair.

Billy stared at nothing, rolling the ice in his glass as a stick smoked between his lips. He didn't notice each side of the table watching and waiting on bated breath. He didn't care.

"I . . . I can't. I can't say yes."

"Why not?" He sank to the floor, watching her eyes shift and lips tense as she finally found him again.

"I love you, Billy. But I'm not in love with you. I never was. I . . . thought I could be. But I can't. My heart . . . doesn't belong to you. And it wouldn't be fair to you if I said yes, only giving you part of me and not all of me. I couldn't live with myself."

She pushed his hand slowly from her lap, folding the ring box closed with a tear-filled sigh. "I'm so sorry, Billy."

"Mr. Hemsworth?"

The sound of his name squinted his eyes as he pulled the cigarette from his mouth, letting the smoke filter out between his lips. "Yes? Yes, the . . . budget."

A woman with a stout build and short brown hair opened the

door to the room and peered in. "Excuse me, Mr. Hemsworth. There's someone here to see you. Says you told him to come as soon as he could? He doesn't have an appointment."

"Thank you, Catherine." Billy placed his glass on the long hardwood table. "We'll continue this meeting at another time."

"If I may, Mr. Hemsworth." The old board member stated.

"No, you may not." Billy glared at him. "We'll reconvene tomorrow at noon."

Everyone stood abruptly, collected their things, and exited the room. Catherine stepped aside and waited for them to leave before ushering in the unexpected guest. Billy turned toward the bar and grabbed a bottle of scotch before pouring it into his glass.

"Mr. Hemsworth." Greenway's familiar voice echoed up into the high ceilings.

"Thank you for coming on such short notice." He turned and held up his half full glass. "May I offer you a drink?"

Greenway wore his staple trench coat and derby, which he plucked from his head. "No. Thank you." He walked into the room toward the table. "I was surprised to get your call."

"It's been a few years." Billy poured the sharp-tasting scotch down his throat. "Tell me, how is your . . . investigation into James Buchanan progressing?"

Greenway folded his hands behind him. "I'm not at liberty to discuss matters of the Bureau's investigations with civilians. Unless . . . there's something you wish to divulge."

Billy clicked the ice in his glass. "There is, but I'll only cooperate if I am given full disclosure on the matter."

"That is a big ask, Mr. Hemsworth."

"Please, call me Will."

"Will." Greenway tilted his chin. "You seem confident as to the weight of the information you carry."

"I am." Billy eyed him carefully. "Do we have an agreement?"

Greenway pushed aside his coat, pulling a cigarette from his coat pocket, "That depends." He lit up, sucking life from the tobacco. "Do you know where he is?"

The corner of Billy's mouth drew up as he emptied the remains of his glass down his throat. Smacking his lips, he placed it back on the table. "No. But I know *how* we can find him."

Acknowledgments

This story is more than JUST a story. It's a love story that symbolically mimics my own (with a few slight adjustments, of course). The time period is one I have been an admirer of for a long, long time. I hope I've done it justice, highlighting a time when the 'perfect life' post war was hiding more than anyone cared to admit.

Thank you to my hubs, who, when I first pitched an idea for a story of Prairie and Marrok (which was so incredibly different), told me it didn't make sense and I should rework the how, when and why. It forced me to think long and hard on how best to showcase these amazing characters, who hold a special place in my heart. This is how they were truly meant to be.

Thanks to all those who supported me throughout this long writing process. To Juliette Caron, my original critique partner and fellow author, who gave me the critical advice I needed to make this story better and let me email her like a crazy person with questions and ideas on a weekly basis. To my friend Katie Judy, who gushed and glowed over this story as much as I had, giving me the confidence to step away from self-publishing to pursue the more frightening world of traditional. To my sensitivity reader, Latisha, who showed me a better way to frame Marrok as not only a strong character, but one with more layers than I was allowing him to possess.

Thank you to my dad, James, for setting up the white screen in our basement to watch the film, *The Wolfman* (1941) on our 8mm reel film projector that planted the seeds of my love and appreciation for classic cinema (and werewolves).

And of course, thank you to Luminary, for seeing the potential in this story and giving it a home. As content as I was to be a self-published author, being chosen by a press was always something I've wanted to achieve. I am so grateful to you and your amazing team.

About The Author

D. Allyson Howlett is a millennial wordsmith from urban Long Island, New York and currently resides in a small farm town with her family in New Hampshire. Her love for werewolves and the supernatural came about when she was 6 years old, watching the 1941 film, *The Wolf Man*, on a vintage 8mm film projector in her parent's basement. *The Moonlight Diner* is her third published novel.